Dana's Duo

A Sexy Romance novella by

Caitlyn Lynch

ISBN: 0-9954466-7-0

ISBN-13: 978-0-9954466-7-0

Scan the QR code below or visit http://eepurl.com/bPAElD to sign up to my mailing list. You'll be notified of my next sizzling hot publication and also get a chance to WIN Amazon gift cards and receive advance reader copies of my books to review!!

CHAPTER ONE

"Thank you, but no."

Graham Harding, the man whose offer of coffee Dana had just turned down, looked completely blank. As though he couldn't comprehend her words. "It's just coffee."

"And I just don't want any. So, thank you for the offer, but no." She turned to walk away, brought up short by the sweating hand that landed firmly on her upper arm.

"Tea?"

"No. Thank you."

The grip tightened, pulling her back to face him. "Why not? I'm in Human Resources, I've seen your file, you said you were unattached. Not *lying* on your intake form, were you, sweetheart?" Graham backed her towards a wall. Dana tried to wrench her arm free of his grip, unsuccessfully. The bastard was strong.

"I wasn't lying," she snapped, by now thoroughly sick of this jerk. "But, you know what? Even single girls have the right to say no."

There was that ridiculously uncomprehending look again, and this time she failed to restrain the impulse to roll her eyes.

"I don't want to get coffee with you. I don't want to go on a date with you. I don't want to sleep with you. I'm not interested." Dana spoke slowly, as though trying to get the message through to a very small child.

"Why not?"

"I don't owe you a reason!" *Because you're short, fat, balding, twice my age and married, you creep!* He wasn't the only one who got to see personnel files. Dana's job in Computer Support meant she had access to nearly all the company's files. After the third time this twit asked her out, she'd checked up on him.

This was the fifth time. Only this time, he'd managed to catch her alone, coming out of the server room in the basement — wait, what was he doing down here anyway? Suddenly, Dana started to feel afraid.

"You're just playing hard to get, you little slut," Graham pushed her back towards the wall — and went flying, his hand ripped off her arm as he was thrown roughly against the opposite wall.

"You ever fucking speak like that to a lady again and I'll hunt you down and carve you into tiny little pieces."

It was the company's Head of Security, Lex Bradshaw, looming over her assailant like some dark angel of mercy. Dana shrank back against the wall, clutching at her arm, a little stunned by how terrifying he looked. Six foot four and about three feet across the shoulders, Lex Bradshaw was rumored to have been a former Navy Seal. She quite believed it. In fact she'd tried to check it out, but his file was almost completely void of information on his background. Which perhaps wasn't surprising, since he was best friends with the company's founder and CEO, Drew Fischer.

"Are you alright, Miss? I heard what he was saying to you." Ignoring Graham for now, Lex turned to look at Dana.

"I'm fine," she gasped, a little stunned at being face to face with the man she'd been crushing on silently for months. She'd never been within ten feet of him before. He was even more gorgeous up close, the company's uniform polo shirt stretched tight over his broad shoulders and thickly muscled biceps, his chiseled cheekbones drawn in sharp relief as he looked down at her with a concerned expression.

"Do you want to press charges?" His tone was calm and even.

Dana thought about it, but in the end shook her head. Graham had a nasty fright, and he was most definitely going to lose his job anyway, because there was an absolute no-harassment policy at the facility, and she now had an unimpeachable witness. She somehow doubted that she'd ever set eyes on the jerk again.

"Get outta my sight," Lex growled, and Graham scraped himself off the floor where he'd been thrown and ran as fast as his chubby little legs would carry him.

Lex turned back to look at Dana again, and to her astonishment lifted gentle fingers to touch her upper arm lightly. "Think you're gonna get a bruise there, doll."

"Oh, I, um, maybe. I'll be fine. It's fine. Really." Oh hell, now she'd been reduced to a stuttering idiot.

"It isn't fine, Miss. Please, I'm happy to escort you to the company medical office, or maybe drive you to your own doctor, or the emergency room," Lex disagreed.

"Dana."

"Hm?" Lex looked confused.

"It's Dana, not Miss. Please."

"Well," his beautiful smile bloomed, throwing his cheekbones into even sharper relief and flashing a completely unexpected dimple in his chin, "in that case, I'm Lex."

She laughed shyly. "I know who you are, sir."

"Lex!"

"Lex." Those blue eyes, *ugh*, he was *devastating*. Dana just stared helplessly up at him. He tilted his head slightly, a black curl tumbling onto his forehead.

"Well, if you won't let me take you to a doctor, would you please come with me to file an internal complaint against Mr Harding? The sooner I have him off the premises the better I'll like it."

"I can do that," she agreed, still dazed by the sheer impact of his good looks in such close proximity. *Her desk neighbor Eleanor was never going to believe this*, Dana thought with an inward smirk. She and Ellie had both been crushing on Lex for months now, ever since they both started work at Fischer Inc's headquarters at the same time.

"Normally it would go through HR, but since Harding works there, I'll handle it personally. Come on up to my office and we'll create the report, and I'll take it straight in to Drew." Lex's fingers curled gently under her elbow, but he didn't pull. Just nudged her gently towards the elevators and waited until she began to move before he started to walk alongside her. "We'll have him off the premises before close of business today, Dana, I promise you."

"I'm not afraid of him," she claimed, though the way she'd felt when she realized Graham had caught her alone in the basement still sent a tiny tremor up her spine.

"I can see that," Lex drawled, amusement in his tone. "You were certainly giving the little creep a good tongue-lashing when I intervened."

"Mom always did say that I could talk my way out of trouble most times," Dana grinned mischievously up at him.

"Most times." Lex looked down at her as they stepped into the elevator. He'd seen her around a few times now, darting in and out of offices, fixing computers and making the place run smoothly. She was probably average height at around five foot six, but that was pretty tiny next to his height. She certainly wasn't fragile, delicious hips curving out her close-fitting black pants and a generous cleavage, of which he was afforded a superb view from his height vantage. He leaned over to punch the button for the executive floor, getting a little closer to Dana.

Dana inhaled, breathing in a disturbingly delicious scent, warm musky male and a very nice cologne. *Oh boy, he smells good.*

"Well, that's very kind of you, Dana," Lex drawled, and to her utmost horror she realized she'd said that last thought *out loud.*

"I'm gonna run away now."

"I don't really think you've got anywhere to go," his firm lips quirked with amusement. "Considering we're in an elevator, and I don't think you should go back to your desk until I've sorted out the Harding situation."

Dana groaned and dropped her head back against the wall of the elevator. "I'll just quietly die of embarrassment right here, then."

Lex moved, and she opened her eyes to find him standing before her, one hand braced on the wall beside her head, his bright blue eyes gleaming down at her. "I'm cool with it. You can sniff on me all you like."

Dana couldn't help a slightly nervous giggle, thinking how very different Lex's light flirting made her feel to Graham's creepy pursuit. *Maybe it was because she only found one of them attractive,* she thought, concentrating on keeping the words to herself this time.

"It's a very nice cologne you're wearing," she admitted.

He smiled, and took his hand off the wall, stepping back as the elevator doors pinged open. He made a gallant gesture for her to go out ahead of him, which she did, but she then wasn't sure which way to turn to get to his office.

"This way," again Lex's fingers brushed very lightly under her elbow, guiding her to turn right. Dana turned, and found herself walking in step with him along a plushly carpeted corridor. He was shortening his steps to walk with her, she realized, and smiled slightly. He might not be HR, but he was still doing a very good job of putting her at her ease.

Except for the fact that his very masculine presence was thoroughly unsettling, and would have been no matter what situation they happened to meet in.

Lex's office was large and surprisingly homely; Dana had somehow expected it to be austere and formal, but there was a large squashy couch to one side as well as a more formal office table and chairs, and a shelf of well-thumbed books beside the desk. He had his own coffee machine, which he set running even before closing the door and gesturing Dana to take a seat before the desk.

"Why don't you tell me, in your own words, just how Graham Harding has been bothering you?" Lex asked quietly, taking his own seat and watching Dana. She looked down at her hands, twisting them together in her lap slightly.

"I suppose it started a few days after I started work, actually."

Lex felt slightly sick when she finished talking. How the hell had he not become aware of this earlier? Working in HR, that asshole had definitely abused his position to harass and pursue Dana, and quite possibly other women as well. Lex didn't care to think about what might have happened if he hadn't spotted Harding going down the stairwell to the basement and followed him out of sheer curiosity as to what business the man might have down there.

"I'm so sorry, Dana," Lex apologized sincerely. "This should never have been allowed to happen. I'm sure you realize that Harding being in HR means he slipped through the cracks…"

"I do, and I don't hold it against Fischer, Inc., honestly!" she lifted large brown eyes to him and nodded earnestly. "I should probably have bypassed him and gone to — to…"

"Me. Security means internal security as well as external. Our people have to feel safe to do their work." Lex finished typing on the form he'd been filling in as they worked, turned his laptop towards Dana. "Have a look through. If you feel it's complete, I can print it out for you to sign."

She had a very adorable habit of nibbling on her lower lip as she read, he noted, winding a long curly strand of brown hair around a slender finger, then unwinding it again. Lex had to wonder how those springy curls would feel in his own fingers, how those plump, soft lips would taste under how own.

Drew will like her, he thought, and grinned to himself. *Drew will like her a lot.*

Dana nodded finally, pushing the laptop back towards him. "Yeah, I'd say that's pretty accurate. Harsh, but true."

"With this on file, you can still press charges if you decide to later," Lex said, hitting keys to print the document out. "Okay. Sign here, please…" he added his own, scrawling signature as witness beneath her own. "All right. Let's go see Drew, he'll tear up Harding's contract and I will take great pleasure in escorting him off the premises personally."

The thought made her smile, and she followed Lex out of the office and just a few steps further along the hallway. A blonde secretary in, Dana estimated, her mid-fifties, looked up and smiled at Lex.

"Is Drew free, Alison?"

"He'd make time for you anyway, but yes. Go right on in." Alison looked curiously at Dana.

"Dana Moretti from Computer Services," Lex introduced her, but didn't say why she was there. A light touch under Dana's elbow guided her forward, and Lex opened the door without knocking and ushered her into the office.

It was a corner office — of course — with the most spectacular view of the city skyline Dana had ever seen. She gaped unprofessionally at the view for a moment, barely noticing the man rising from his desk to greet them. Until he stepped closer and her eyes snapped to him, taking in his height and good looks.

Drew Fischer was the light to Lex Bradshaw's dark, blond where his friend was fair, clean-shaven while Lex rocked a more bad-boy six o'clock shadow. To make a judgment call on which of them was better-looking was way beyond the ability of mere mortals, Dana decided, looking from one to the other of them in something of an overwhelmed daze.

Drew looked at Lex curiously before turning his attention to Dana, taking her in with a long look of masculine appreciation, though he spent most of the stare on her face and she didn't feel in any way creeped out by the attention.

"Lex?" Drew said at last, questioningly.

"This is Dana Moretti, Drew; she's a very capable technician from our Computer Support division, and I've just discovered that she's been having a major harassment problem with Graham Harding from HR."

Drew's casual demeanor underwent a sharp change; his pleasant smile vanished, replaced with a look of horror. "What? My God!" Looking back at Dana, he gestured to a grouping of comfortable chairs near the window. "Please, Dana, have a seat and tell me about what's been happening and what we can do to help."

"I've already got it under control, Drew," Lex said, though yet another of those light touches on Dana's elbow told her that she should sit where Drew had invited her. Lex held out the papers he was holding and Drew accepted them. "I witnessed a pretty ugly incident quite by chance. We've got all the details down there; I just need your countersignature and I'll go escort Harding out of the building."

Drew didn't even bother to read the paperwork, just plucked a pen from the breast pocket of his shirt and signed on the last page. Dana realized he must have absolute trust in Lex. "There you go, buddy. Get him out of the building. Dana can stay safely here with me until he's gone."

With a nod, Lex left them, and Drew took a seat opposite Dana, smiling at her warmly. It was kind of like being bathed in sunlight, she thought inconsequentially, then realized he'd asked her something. "Sorry, what?"

"Would you like some coffee?"

"Oh, no. Thanks. I'm good."

Dana sat there feeling awkward while Drew made small talk. He was obviously trying to put her at ease, but she was entirely aware that she was only in his office because of something that had gone wrong at his company. He was probably hoping to avoid a lawsuit. So she made vague responses to his polite conversation, trying not to look at him, at the concern in his blue eyes. When Lex returned she jumped gratefully to her feet.

"He's gone? Good. I really have to get back to work. Servers won't look after themselves, you know."

Lex and Drew shared a look she didn't see, and then Lex said; "That's fine, Dana. Will you do something for me, though? Just program my personal number into your phone, and call me if you have any more trouble."

She agreed to that, fished out her phone and programmed in the number he dictated to her.

"Any problems, Dana, please call," he said, his voice quite gentle.

"Thanks, I will!" She offered him and Drew a distracted smile and hurried out.

"What did you say to her?" Lex asked the moment the door closed.

"Nothing!" Drew stood up to pace, running a hand through his hair distractedly. "She's gorgeous, but I was hardly going to make a move right now, when she'd just been harassed by another employee!"

"All right, all right. Cool your jets." Lex put a steadying hand on Drew's shoulder. "We don't even know if she'd be open to the suggestion. We'll give things a couple days to settle and then I'll 'drop by' and check up on her."

Drew sighed, puffed out his cheeks. Looked at his best friend with a wry grin. "Jeez, man, you really threw me for a loop there for a minute. When I saw you come in with her, I thought for a moment I was getting an early birthday present or something."

Lex's blue eyes went very wide before he started to laugh. "Ever the optimist."

Drew gave him a wry look, and Lex leaned in to kiss him. "Soon. I hope. I liked her very much and I knew you would too, but I don't think she's the kind of girl we want to rush."

"I hate you when you're right," but Drew turned to face him, slipping his arms around Lex's lean waist.

"I'm usually right."

"I know, you asshole!"

DANA'S DUO

CHAPTER TWO

Fishing her keys from the satchel she used as an oversized purse, Dana opened the front door of her apartment building and stepped into the side hallway to check her mailbox.

"Evening, Mrs Chao," she said to the elderly lady in there with her.

"Oh, Dana, hello, dear. I just sent your boyfriend up to your apartment. I thought you'd be back already and maybe hadn't heard the bell."

"Uh," Dana blinked at her. "My boyfriend?"

"Yes, he was just waiting at the door when I got here." Mrs Chao looked her up and down, shook her head, and said "There's no accounting for taste, but I'd have thought a pretty girl like you could do better than *that*." With that, she shuffled out, and Dana was left with a horrible sinking feeling in her stomach.

Unsure of what to do, she pulled out her phone and stared at it a moment. *Should I call the police?* That felt like a massive over-reaction. *Lex,* she thought then. *Lex won't think I'm over-reacting.* She tapped the screen to dial his number before she could second-guess herself.

"Lex Bradshaw," his deep voice rumbled after only a single ring.

"Uh, hi, it's Dana Moretti. You said I could call if anything happened…"

"What is it, Dana?" his voice sharpened. "Where are you? What's the problem?"

"I just got back to my apartment building and one of my neighbors said she sent my boyfriend up to my apartment, only I don't have a boyfriend, and… I might be over-reacting but I have this terrible feeling that it's Graham Harding." She was gabbling, she realized, tried to steady her voice.

"Get out of there right now." Lex's voice was calm, but commanding, and Dana found herself hurrying for the front door. "I want you to go somewhere safe but close by, Dana, somewhere with lots of people. There a Starbucks or anything near you?"

"There's a burger joint on the next block." She knew it would be buzzing at this time of the evening.

"Go there and wait. I'm on my way to you. Won't be long. Stay on the line and keep talking to me until you get there, Dana, okay?"

She should have felt frightened, considering what his words implied, but his low voice was quite steady, making her feel confident and grounded. She walked to the burger joint, talking all the way, answering his routine questions about what she'd been doing that afternoon.

"I'm here," she said at last. "There's loads of people."

"Go on in and wait. Sit somewhere well away from the window. I'll be about ten minutes."

To her immense surprise, when a gleaming black Mercedes pulled up outside, it wasn't only Lex who got out, but also Drew Fischer.

"Dana," Lex smiled down at her gently. "I need you to go with Drew for now, and give me your keys. The police are meeting me at your apartment building."

"Now I *do* feel like I've over-reacted," Dana said, "what if it's not even him?"

"Sh," Lex put the tip of his finger very gently against her lips, shaking his head. "You're not over-reacting. Give me your keys."

"Let us take care of it, Dana," Drew put in quietly. "Please. We don't want you to have to see him. It's a potentially dangerous situation."

"How could it be dangerous?" She shook her head, smiling with disbelief.

"He owns a gun." Lex's voice was flat.

Shocked, Dana stared at him wide-eyed.

"Give him your keys, Dana," Drew told her gently, and this time she didn't argue, dipping into her satchel and handing them over with shaking fingers.

"Please be careful?" she begged Lex. He smiled, showing that unexpected dimple in his chin again.

"Don't worry about me, angel. Go with Drew now and I'll let you know when it's safe for you to come home."

Dana let Drew take her arm and lead her out to the waiting car; he opened the rear door to let her in and slid in after her. The uniformed driver immediately drove away without waiting for direction so Dana supposed it was already agreed.

"Where are we going?" she asked in a small voice.

"A hotel not too far from here that I have a part ownership in," Drew said, his voice reassuring. "It has a nice quiet restaurant. We'll go and have something to eat and Lex will let us know when it's safe for me to take you home."

"This is so kind of you," her voice shook a little. "I've probably wrecked your plans for the evening, I'm sorry to be so much trouble."

"It's no hardship at all to have dinner with a lovely woman, I assure you," Drew's voice carried a hint of laughter. "Quite the opposite."

That made Dana smile a little too, and when they pulled up in the hotel's portico and Drew slipped out to hold the door open for her, she stepped out and smiled up at him properly, a hint of sass in the expression.

"Just as long as you're paying, because with what you're paying me, I don't think I can afford this place."

Drew laughed, rich and full, and offered her his arm. "Buying you dinner is absolutely the least I can do. Order whatever you like, up to and including the best from their wine cellar."

"You might regret that offer," she warned cheekily, making him chuckle again.

"Never. I promise."

Dana might have felt a little self-conscious walking into the swanky hotel in her plain blouse and slacks from work, except that Drew never gave her a chance. He fit right in with his perfectly tailored suit, of course, and the staff clearly recognized him because within moments they were swept to a discreetly placed table in a side alcove, with a nice view of the dining room. Menus were presented, fresh iced water poured, and then they were left alone, leaving Dana wondering if some kind of magic had just occurred. Drew was clearly taking it all for granted, opening the menu to peruse it thoughtfully.

"Would you like some wine?" he glanced up at Dana over the menu.

"Okay," she shrugged. Considering her slightly frazzled nerves, a glass of wine or two would probably be a great relaxant.

"Any preference?"

"Whatever you think. Any wine I drink is normally out of the bargain bin," she confessed, making Drew chuckle quietly. He gestured to a hovering server and placed an order for something which sounded French; it had *chateau* in the name, anyway.

Dana really didn't feel up to eating much, so she ordered some soup and a salad, figuring that she could probably manage to get some soup down and then at least pick at the salad. The food was so beautifully presented, and tasted so good when it arrived, though, that she ended up eating every last bite.

"Dessert?" Drew offered with some amusement, watching Dana lick the last droplet of salad dressing off her lips with a satisfied sigh. She was absolutely delightful, loosening up as the meal progressed and he deliberately kept the conversation light, asking innocuous questions about her background, her education, her chosen career, sharing a few light-hearted snippets about himself in return.

"Oh," Dana pushed a hand through her curly hair and smiled at him, "I probably shouldn't. Won't be good for my waistline."

"Your waistline is absolutely perfect," Drew said without thinking, and she blushed a little, gave him a pert grin.

"Well, that's very kind of you to say!"

"Trust me, I couldn't help but notice." Even in the sensible flat shoes she was wearing, her walk was very womanly, her hips swaying. When she left the table for a few moments to visit the bathroom, Drew had been so hypnotized by the back view as she walked away that he'd missed his mouth with his fork. Twice.

Is he flirting with me? Dana couldn't quite believe it, but the warm, appreciative look Drew was giving her was quite unmistakable. There was nothing impersonal about the expression; she'd go so far as to call it *bedroom eyes*, actually. Casting her own eyes down in some confusion, she murmured;

"Well, maybe I will have something. I'm sure their desserts are as fabulous as everything else."

Drew suspected he was making her a little uncomfortable, but he couldn't help watching her as she ate the honeycomb-laced chocolate cheesecake she finally selected, her unpainted lips pursing as she sucked the gooey treat off her spoon in a way that made his throat dry. He shifted a little uncomfortably in his seat, trying to ease the constriction his suit pants were putting on his arousal. His phone vibrated in his pants pocket and he almost jumped out of his seat with a very unmanly squeak.

Glancing at Dana, seeing that she was still absorbed in her dessert, Drew carefully slid the phone from his pocket and glanced at it. Lex had been a long time; Drew had honestly expected him to turn up by the time the main courses were served and join them.

We had trouble. On my way now, the text message read. Drew suppressed the urge to text back asking if Lex was all right. The other man could more than handle himself. Instead, he suggested to Dana that they move into the hotel's comfortable coffee lounge once she'd finished eating. She looked as though she was about to ask questions, but bit her lip after a moment and nodded.

Their coffee had just been delivered when Lex arrived, striding in and coming straight over to them. He looked serious and Dana swallowed down a lump in her throat. Standing up, she smoothed her hands nervously over the front of her slacks.

"What — what happened?" she asked, sensed rather than saw Drew standing up behind her, moving in close, a silently supportive presence at her back.

"I think you should probably sit down, Dana," Lex's voice was gentle, despite his serious expression.

"Tell me!" her hands fisted at her sides.

"Harding had broken into your apartment," Lex said it baldly at last, watched her sway slightly, her face paling. "He didn't have his gun — he hadn't been home, we think — but he'd taken knives from your kitchen and slashed up your bed. He was waiting there for you."

Drew's hands landed on Dana's waist then, supporting her lightly. Lex stepped in a little closer, lifted both hands to frame her cheeks gently, bending down close so his forehead almost touched hers. "You're safe, angel. I promise. He made the incredibly dumb mistake of attacking one of the police officers, managed to nick her arm. He'll see jail for that at the very least, but you have to press charges for the harassment now, do you see?"

She nodded dumbly, tears welling in her eyes.

"Hush." Lex pressed his lips gently against her forehead. "I've got two of my people at your apartment right now. They're gonna get rid of the slashed mattress, put a new door and some new locks on." His eyes above Dana's head met Drew, and the other man's lips thinned as he read Lex's expression correctly; there was a lot more mess that Lex hadn't told Dana about that needed to be cleaned up.

"Th-thank you," Dana whimpered, and Lex groaned.

"Don't thank me. If I'd had a better handle on what that asshole was like, you wouldn't be in this situation now! I'm fucking kicking myself."

"You and me both," Drew said, "because I hired the bastard in the first place."

Dana shook her head, absolving both of them of blame. Drew was holding her against him supportively, the back of her head and her shoulders resting against his chest; with Lex standing close in front of her she felt surrounded by them, but far from being overwhelmed she felt warm and incredibly safe.

"It's not either of your fault, and it's not mine, either," she said firmly, looking up into Lex's bright blue eyes, finding a smile from somewhere for him. "Thank you, though, for everything you've done."

"Dana," Lex shook his head, grinning. "It's nothing. I'd like to do a lot more than that for you. Hell, we both would."

There was an instant of ringing silence as Dana digested what he'd just said. Blinked.

Drew's hands dropped from her waist and he moved back, giving her space. Lex let go of her too, took a small step back. Drew moved around to stand shoulder to shoulder with him, both of them watching her in silence, waiting for her response.

Dana looked up at them, at the intense looks they were both giving her. Gulped.

"B-both of you?"

"We do everything together," Lex said, and the look he gave her, his eyes sweeping down to her toes and back up again, made it very clear what he was thinking about *doing.*

"You... do?" Dana had heard speculation that they occasionally shared a bedroom, but nobody knew for sure, and they didn't display anything more than friendly affection in public.

"We'd sure like to," Drew affirmed, and he was giving her a look that was just as heated, just as masculine.

I'm hallucinating, aren't I? I fell and hit my head and I'm having a really, really amazing dream.

"Nope."

"Oh shit I said that out loud!"

They were both grinning, moving closer again. "Could be more than just an amazing dream, angel," Lex brushed his fingers lightly down her jawline. "Could be the best night of your life."

"I really must be dreaming," Dana said, staring up at him dazedly, "because there's no way either of you would ever want me, never mind *both* of you."

"Whatever makes you say that?" Drew moved in closer on her other side, his hand curving lightly around her wrist before he lifted her hand and pressed a slow, moist kiss to the back of it. "Lex and I have had our eyes on you for a while."

"Wanted to do much more'n just look, too," Lex's fingers slipped down to caress lightly at her neck. "Wanted to touch, but we figured a girl like you would've been snapped up long ago, and we weren't gonna poach on another guy's patch."

Dana started looking around.

"What are you looking for?" Drew asked, following her gaze and frowning as he realized she wasn't really looking at anything.

"The portal to the parallel dimension I've clearly fallen through."

That made both of them laugh. Drew let go of her wrist, and as though at an unspoken signal, Lex dropped his hand from her face and they both took a step back.

"This is the real world, Dana." It was Drew who spoke, his face serious. "The choice is yours. You're the kind of girl Lex and I have dreamed about sharing, but… I understand that it's a pretty extreme idea, both of us at once."

"It's a really *hot* idea," she said without stopping to consider how they'd take that.

"In the abstract or as in, you'd like to find out?" Lex's voice had lowered, deepened, as he gazed down at her, his eyelids drooping a little.

Dana swallowed, licked her lips. *I'd be mad to turn this offer down. I'd regret it for the rest of my life.* "I think I'd very much like to find out."

Surprisingly, it was Drew who leaned in to kiss her first, considering the way Lex had been looking at her. Drew's mouth was hot, hungry as he hauled her against him, and then suddenly Lex was there behind her, sandwiching her between two massive, hard bodies, Lex's mouth hot on her neck as he pressed his face in, nipping and licking as the sensitive flesh.

Drew's kiss was far more demanding than she'd expected, his tongue urgent as he thrust it between her lips to taste her mouth, his strong hands on her waist holding her close. Dana was quickly getting a crick in her neck, though, and tried to pull back. Drew made a little growling noise, seeking to keep kissing her, but she got a hand on his chest and pressed lightly.

"Wait."

Lex lifted his head with a reluctant grumble. "Why?"

"Because this isn't the best place or time." The coffee lounge was empty except for the three of them, but she was suddenly all too conscious that someone could walk in at any time, and the position the three of them were in couldn't be construed as anything other than extremely compromising.

"Ehhhh," Drew grinned ruefully, reluctantly moving back a little. "Damn, she's right, Lex."

"Ugh," Lex moved back too, and Dana shivered, suddenly cold with the loss of their warm bodies against hers. They were both still staring at her with heated eyes, making goosebumps spring up all over her skin. "Our timing's crappy, isn't it, angel? After Harding being such a fucking creepy stalker to you today."

Dana shook her head. "I don't care about that. It doesn't matter. I meant, just — not here." She gestured her hand to indicate the coffee lounge.

"Don't go home," Lex said quietly. "My people are securing it, but I don't want you there alone tonight. Come to our place."

Dana had already made her mind up, so she nodded. Accepted Drew's hand as he offered it, let him lead her out to the waiting car. Inside, sandwiched between two sets of broad shoulders, Dana found her breathing coming fast, her palms beginning to sweat. Drew's hand touched hers lightly, drew small circles on the back of it. He smiled when she looked up at him.

"We don't have to do anything you don't want to," Drew assured quietly, and the calm sincerity in his gray-blue eyes had Dana nodding, accepting that they wouldn't push for more than she was happy to give.

CHAPTER THREE

It wasn't long before they arrived at an apartment building in a very different part of the city to Dana's, a glamorous place with a dress circle address and a uniformed doorman who buzzed them in upon seeing Drew and Lex.

Even the elevator was unexpected; there weren't even any call buttons, just a scanner panel. Drew's palm on the panel caused the steel doors to slide noiselessly open, though, and then the elevator zoomed all three of them up to what Dana suspected was the building's top floor, even though once again there were no buttons inside the elevator, no way to tell how many floors there actually were.

The elevator doors opened onto a small foyer, a single, ornately carved timber door opposite. This one didn't even have a lock on it, just what appeared to be a fingerprint scanner, which Drew again activated.

"This way," Lex's hand landed on the small of her back, and he guided her gently through the door as Drew held it open.

Dana looked around curiously as she entered the apartment, wondering who it actually belonged to. But then Drew had said 'our place', did the two men live together? The furniture looked old – as in *antique* – but comfortable and lived-in. Through an open door she glimpsed a huge bed – was that actually a four-poster? Taking a tentative step forward, she peered in that direction.

"That's where we're headed, angel," Lex's voice was low and rasping, his blue eyes, when Dana looked around, intent on her.

"But we should be good hosts and ask first if you're hungry or thirsty?" Drew asked, turning back towards her as he finished closing the door.

Shaking her head, Dana stood twisting her hands together in front of her, a little nervous. "No… no, that dinner was more than enough for me."

"Good," Lex had moved closer, stood right behind her, his breath warm on her neck. "Think I'd go mad if I had to wait too long."

Turning to look at him, she smiled seductively. "You don't have to wait at all."

Bright blue eyes darkened, and he slipped one strong arm around her waist, pulling her close before he bent his head.

Dana had dreamed about Lex Bradshaw's mouth. It was far too sensual for a man, plush pink lips — and he did seem to have an inordinately distracting habit of licking his lips. He licked them now just before kissing her, his mouth warm and sweet-tasting, the kiss hungry, his stubble rasping lightly on her tender skin.

"Damn," she heard Drew murmur distantly, and Lex laughed softly against her mouth before lifting his head. They both looked at Drew to find him standing staring, hand pressed against his groin, his expression aroused.

"Come on over here," Dana invited with a coy little smile, feeling suddenly emboldened by the way both men were looking at her, "better yet, let's take all this into the bedroom — eek!" Lex had scooped her off her feet and carried her into the bedroom, tossing her onto the bed. She bounced with an indignant squeal.

"Lex, you jerk, that's no way to treat a lady!" Drew reproached sternly.

Dana laughed up at them both. "Would a *lady* be here agreeing to be with both of you, Drew? Would a lady do this?" Reaching up, she unfastened the top button of her blouse. Two pairs of eyes riveted on her, two broad chests inflated with deep breaths as she moved down and unfastened another button. *Thank goodness it was laundry day yesterday and she was wearing her best undies,* Dana thought. Pretty lace peeped out from the gap as her blouse parted.

"Feelin' kinda lonely over here all on my lonesome, fellas," she offered up a winning smile, and they moved both together, almost in perfect sync, reaching the bed in a couple of quick strides. Lex stopped to kick his boots off while Drew peeled his shirt off over his head even as he sat down on the bed.

"You're beautiful," it was Drew who spoke, but the look in Lex's eyes said the exact same thing as he wrenched his shirt off, throwing it carelessly aside. Dana's eyes fastened with shock on his scars, on roughened, reddened flesh across the left side of his chest.

"Oh," Lex made to turn away, his right hand coming up to press over the scars. "I'm sorry, it's so ugly…"

"Lex!" Going to her knees, she reached out imploringly to him. "Don't, please. I want you. Scars and all. I didn't know about them, but they don't make a difference to me, I promise."

From the corner of her eye, she saw Drew's smile. "Told ya, Lex. Told you she wouldn't judge you by it. She's not that kind of girl, are you, beautiful?"

"Definitely not." Lex still stood hesitant at the end of the bed, so she crawled towards him, aware that her breasts were definitely showing to advantage as her blouse gaped open. Lex's lips parted, a flush rising on his high cheekbones as Dana went to him, kneeling upright at the end of the bed, lifting a hand to brush lightly over the ridged, scarred flesh on his chest.

"It's part of you," she told him quietly, eyes locked with his, seeing his pupils dilate as she spoke. "It's a war wound, isn't it? You're a hero, Lex. I'm honored that you want me, and your scars don't change a thing about that."

Still he hesitated, until Dana took hold of his hand and tugged gently. He let her lift it, but still stood motionless, at least until she brought it to her mouth and sucked two fingers inside, still watching him.

Lex drew in a sharp breath. "*Fuck*, babe," he muttered on the exhale.

"Do you like this?" Dana whispered around his fingers, flicking her tongue in between them, sucking from root to tip, hollowing her cheeks.

"Damn, yeah!" A grin quirked up one corner of his mouth. "Still, I'd rather you sucked something else."

"Oh, I can do that," letting his fingers out of her mouth regretfully, Dana reached for his belt. His black dress pants were tight enough that she could see clearly how hard he was beneath – and that he was *big*, thick and long.

Lex's grin widened as she unfastened the belt and his pants, pushed them down off his hips along with the plain black jockey shorts he had on underneath. His cock sprang free, pointing eagerly towards her, and she leaned in, opening her mouth for a quick lick around the tip. Lex's cock was thick enough that it was a slightly uncomfortable stretch for her lips to take him in, but she wasn't going to let that stop her.

"Ah, angel," strong fingers caressed gently under her jaw as his other hand slid into her hair. "You're so fucking beautiful like that."

Dana had almost forgotten Drew's presence, he'd been so quiet, until she felt him move on the bed, kneeling behind her. His hands slipped around to her waist and she felt him unfastening the remaining buttons on her blouse, slipping it from her shoulders. In short order her bra followed so she was naked to the waist, and then Drew's big, warm hands were cupping her breasts, tweaking and teasing her nipples as he pressed slow, hot kisses on her shoulder.

Lex was making low, hungry sounds in his throat, as her head bobbed, taking him deep into her mouth with each pass. Her hands were braced on the sides of his legs, holding herself steady as she licked and sucked all over him, tonguing up the little dribbles of pre-cum that gathered in the slit at the tip of his cock.

"Damn, but you're good," Lex breathed it, his breath coming in short pants, his eyes closed. "Feels *so* good."

Dana hummed deliberately, letting her throat tremor, smirked around him as he let out a muffled shout, fingers tightening in her hair briefly.

"Wicked woman," Drew chuckled quietly behind her, and she realized he was watching Lex's face. "He's close," it was a quiet warning, and Dana nodded to show her understanding, but didn't pull off.

"Ahhhh, angel," it was a long, drawn-out moan from Lex, and she felt the pulse through her lips, swallowed hard as he came down her throat —

good grief, there was a *lot* of that, almost choking her. Swallowing again quickly, she pulled back, devoting a good minute to licking him clean, slow delicate licks as he caressed her hair slowly. She was in no hurry to move, not with Drew's hands doing their work, teasing her nipples, sometimes gentle, sometimes tugging on them almost roughly.

At last, Lex sighed and moved back before bending down to kiss her, obviously not caring about the taste of him in her mouth. He smiled directly into her eyes before looking behind her at Drew.

"This beautiful lady ain't having fun yet, you ass."

"Oh, but I am," Dana disagreed at once, glancing down to where Drew's hands had never ceased playing with her breasts. Her nipples stood out stiff and distended, and Lex hummed with pleasure at the sight before reaching out to grasp her waist gently.

"Let's get you more comfortable, angel."

"Do you mean naked?" she asked cheekily as he lifted and Drew pulled, tugging her back on the bed to lay on top of him, her head resting on his thick pectoral muscles. "Because I like the sound of that."

Drew chuckled in her ear, his hands still busy with her breasts, tugging a little more sharply at her nipples, making her arch and gasp. "Cheeky little minx." He pulled and pinched at her nipples as Lex stripped the rest of her clothes away, spreading her legs apart over Drew's.

"So pretty," Lex murmured, and suddenly his tongue was *there*, playing with her clit, the added sensation on top of what Drew was doing almost too much, too intense. Dana flung out her hands, desperate for something to cling to, and Lex caught her hands in his, holding them firmly as his tongue worked.

It was mere moments before the climax hit, arching her up off Drew, hoarse cries spilling from her lips as her whole body tremored. Lex made a pleased humming sound against her and kept licking, gentling his strokes as she got sensitive.

"Feel good, beautiful?" Drew murmured softly. "You feel amazing." His hands gentled on her breasts, too, fingertips just flicking over her aching nipples. Dana could only get out a moan in response as Lex worked on her clit softly.

"What do you want, beautiful?" Drew asked quietly as she writhed atop him.

"Want — want to be fucked. You," she could feel him hard against her ass through his pants. "Want you to fuck me. Fill me. Please."

He let out a soft huff of breath, and Dana felt rather than heard Lex chuckle against her before he moved back.

"Girl's reading your mind, Drew." He was tracing around her clit with a fingertip, occasionally pinching lightly between finger and thumb, making her arch again, broken, strangled sounds spilling from her lips.

"Like you don't want to fuck her senseless as well," vaguely Dana heard Drew jibe back, and then he released her breasts, lifted her off him in one smooth easy movement.

Dana protested — right up until a long finger slid up inside her. "Oh my God."

Lex laughed huskily, and she realized he was watching her, his blue eyes bright, his curly black hair hanging in them slightly, his full lips glistening. Drew, standing just behind him, was yanking his pants off.

Dana really didn't know where to look. There was just too much goodness to feast her eyes on. Drew was all light and brightness, blond hair and golden skin, Lex his hard-edged, darker shadow. Lex solved the conundrum by thrusting another finger deep inside her, making her squeal with ecstasy, her eyes drifting closed despite how very much she wanted to keep looking.

The mattress sank beside Dana and she heard a rip, fought her heavy eyelids open enough to look over and see Drew sitting up against the headboard, rolling a condom on as he avidly watched Lex fingering her.

"Come here and ride me, beautiful," he requested huskily, holding a big hand out towards her.

"Yes," she agreed breathily, tried to scrabble her way towards him, eyes fixed on his cock, swollen and hard as he gave it a few lazy strokes.

"You want this? Come and get it," Drew invited with a wicked smirk.

"Uhhhh," she had to pull herself off Lex's fingers to do that, and she really didn't want to, but oh, that cock looked so tempting… Lex laughed and withdrew his hand.

"She's enjoying herself too much, Drew. Make sure you give her a damn good time, now."

It took a moment for Dana to get her shaking limbs back under control, but then she rolled over and crawled towards Drew, looking up at him through her lashes.

"You want some of this booty?" she grinned cheekily, straddling his muscled thighs, leaning in for a kiss, remembering too late that her mouth would still taste of Lex's come.

Which Drew obviously liked. He licked into her mouth eagerly, making delighted little sounds, his hands settling on her hips to guide her closer, hips rocking so that his cock rubbed along her cleft, chafing on her clit in a way that made her moan into his mouth and grind back hard against him.

"Fuuuck," it was a strangled gasp from Lex that made Dana pull back and look around. He was stripping rapidly, eyes fixed on her sitting on Drew's lap.

And rather to her surprise, he was already hard again, taking his cock in hand once he had his clothes completely off and stroking it, watching the pair of them.

It was a very pretty sight, one Dana found it very hard to tear her eyes away from, remembering how Lex had tasted in her mouth. Reclining on the bed beside Drew, he lay there watching, stroking his cock slowly, thoughtfully.

"Why do I have the feeling that I don't have your full attention?" Drew quipped then, rolling his hips in a slow circle, rubbing the tip of his cock around Dana's entrance and making her gasp and return her attention to him. He was just as beautiful as Lex, day to the other man's night, blond hair falling over one blue-green eye as he looked up at her.

"You've got my full attention," Dana gasped as the thick, flared head of his cock nudged inside her.

"Good. Wouldn't want you to get distracted, now."

He was lowering her as he spoke, his cock sliding deep into her soaked depths, his voice getting a little tighter, which was good. She wouldn't want to think that he was unaffected, because she sure as hell was, her eyes just about rolling back in her head at how good he felt pushing deep, deep inside her.

"Omigod, oh *Drew*," Dana scrabbled at his shoulders, digging her nails in, clinging to him as he easily lifted and lowered her on his rock-hard cock.

Suddenly there were hands cupping her breasts again, Lex, kneeling beside both of them, tweaking her nipples until she gasped before he leaned in and took one of them into his heated mouth, suckling hard.

Wracking tremors kept rippling through her whole body, tightening her down on Drew as he thrust, making him groan deep in his chest.

"That's it," he gasped, "oh yes, ahhh, so good, beautiful… want to feel you come on me. Please." He gazed at her, his eyes bright behind a thick fringe of golden lashes, looking so immaculate – Dana had a sudden urge to mess him up, shoved her fingers into his thick blond hair to ruffle it, scratch at his scalp. He groaned and pushed up into her fingers, eyes closing and lips parting, so she leaned in and gave him another filthy kiss, all teeth and tongue, rolling her hips hard to grind his cock deep inside her.

Lex's teeth tugged at her nipple, making her shudder then, and his hand slid in between her and Drew to finger at her clit.

"Soaked," he murmured, pulling his mouth from her breast. "Fucking soaked, you like this? Does he feel good, inside you?"

"So good," was about all Dana could pant as he rubbed her clit faster, matching Drew's rhythm of thrusts. "So *aaah!*"

"That's it," Drew growled out, jerking his hips faster, his fingers digging lightly into her hips, "come on, sweetheart, come for me, want to feel it *oh yes!*"

Dana couldn't have held it back even if she'd wanted to, not with Lex suckling on one nipple, his fingers playing the other as his other hand worked her clit and Drew's thick cock pistoned hard inside her, rubbing right over her G-spot with every long stroke. Letting her head fall back, she shrieked with ecstasy, her whole body shaking hard.

"Oh God! Oh God," she collapsed onto Drew's broad chest, and he chuckled, rubbing her back gently.

"My name's Drew," he chided gently.

"Unf. You're lucky I can remember *my* name, never mind yours, after *that*," she mumbled against his neck.

Lex laughed. "She's got you there."

"Obviously we're not trying hard enough, if she can still remember her own name, though."

Something unspoken passed between the two men, and then Dana felt Lex's hand on her back, stroking gently down her spine.

"Dana."

"Ummm."

His fingers trailed lower, caressed over her buttocks, as he leant in and pressed slow kisses against her shoulder.

"We want to share you."

"Yeah…" her brain was really pretty scrambled right then, but she lifted her head, blinked at him slowly. "Yeah?"

"Think you can take both of us?" His eyes gleamed at her, one dark brow quirking.

"Both – together?" It wasn't something she'd ever tried. But certainly she was aware of the possibility. Had even – maybe – woken once or twice from a dream of doing that exact thing. With these two men.

Once again, Dana had to consider the possibility that she was actually dreaming right at that moment. But she didn't think she could have ever dreamed how good Drew felt inside her. How ridiculously turned on she felt.

"Yes," she gasped in answer to Lex's inquiring glance. "Yes, yes I want it, I want you, I want you *both*."

He nodded, eyes never leaving hers, before reaching over to the nightstand and fishing in the open drawer there. Pulling out another condom packet – and a bottle of lube.

Oh – that was probably a good idea. Dana watched avidly as he rolled the condom on before slicking his fingers and moving to kneel behind her. Drew parted his knees to make room for Lex, spreading her a little further open, making her gasp as his rigid erection shifted inside her.

"Play with her clit while I open her up, Drew," Lex ordered, "make sure Dana's having a good time."

"Oh, I'm pretty sure she's having a good time, aren't you, beautiful?" Drew murmured, but he did as Lex said and eased a big hand down, scissoring two fingers lightly over her clit.

"Yes," she panted, a little mewl escaping her as she felt one of Lex's wet fingers press against the tight ring of her ass. "Yes, oh God, oh yes, *hnnnggghh*!"

"Easy," Lex kissed her shoulder and neck slowly, wet open-mouthed kisses, as his finger eased slowly in. "Just relax into it."

"That's – easy for – you to say!" Dana panted. It was difficult not to writhe on Drew, but that would make what Lex was doing feel even more intense, so she clung to him instead, pressing her damp brow against his collarbone.

"Sshh," one strong hand rubbed at the back of her neck, a finger circled her clit lightly, and Lex eased another finger in.

It took a few moments for Dana to realize that the low, wordless moan was coming from her throat. But it was a moan of ecstasy, not pain, and both men recognized that. Lex bit down lightly on her shoulder as his fingers scissored apart, moving more easily now as the muscle relaxed, and she moaned louder and shuddered against him.

"You're close, aren't you?" Drew murmured, easing his fingers off her clit. She sobbed with the loss, making him chuckle huskily.

"Not yet, beautiful."

Dana loved the way he called her that. It made her *feel* beautiful, desirable. His warm lips sought hers, kissed her hungrily as Lex's delving fingers opened her wider. It felt painful and wonderful all at the same time as Lex worked slowly, his hot mouth lavishing kisses down her spine all the while.

"Please," she begged finally, tearing her mouth from Drew's. "Please, Lex!"

He laughed huskily in response, moved closer, slipping his fingers out of her. Drew grinned. "Eager, beautiful?"

"Mm," she had come down away from that sharp edge of pleasure, but he was still thick and hard and hot inside her, pressing on some extremely good spots. "Aaah!" her back arched as Lex pressed against her, the thick, latex-sheathed head of his cock squeezing slowly past the tight muscle of her ass.

"Okay, beautiful?" it was Drew who checked, Lex was making eager panting sounds behind her and Dana suspected that probably felt as good to him as it did to her.

"Yes… yes, just… s-s-slow," she gasped as Lex edged a little deeper before pulling back a fraction.

"Oh, angel," warm lips caressed the back of her neck, his stubble rasping a little on her skin, making goose-bumps flare up. "You feel so good. Just wanna slam home and make you scream."

"Behave, you jerk," Drew's voice was amused, but a little strained, and Dana realized she must be tightening on him as Lex filled her up.

"Says the man who's already balls-deep," she gasped, making both of them chuckle and causing Dana to let out a little squeal as they shifted inside her.

"You're sassy, I like it," Lex nipped at the back of her neck, pressing a little deeper. "Bad girl."

"If this is what bad girls get I'm gonna misbehave all the *oh God yes, please, please, Drew! Lex!*" her voice rose to a shriek as Drew rolled his hips, pressing up into her and pushing her back hard onto Lex's cock at the same time. Lex slid deep with a sudden rush and she lost her mind completely, thrashing and clawing at Drew's shoulders as Lex's hands tightened over her breasts.

"Holy fucking shit!" Drew roared out as she came *hard*, tightening convulsively on both of them, and Lex growled wordlessly, biting down roughly on her shoulder.

"Don't stop," Dana managed to pant somehow in between cries of ecstasy, and they took her at her word, both of them moving, fucking her through it, keeping her at the crest of pleasure for longer than she'd ever have thought possible. And then, as she came down, pushing her back up again, and *again*, until she was just a sobbing, pleasure-wracked mess in between the two of them.

Finally Drew let go his own control, surged inside her with a shout, and Lex followed scant seconds later, both of them pulsing hotly together inside her.

Utterly wrung out, exhausted, Dana collapsed limply to the bed as they both eased carefully out. Barely conscious, she was nonetheless aware of them gently arranging her limbs in a comfortable position, one of them carefully wiping her down with a warm wet cloth as the other smoothed her hair, low masculine voices praising her softly as they curled up on either side of her, a delicious sandwich of masculine muscle.

It felt warm and comfortable and so *safe* lying in between the two of them, that Dana couldn't make her eyes open, couldn't make her mouth work to speak. They seemed to understand how she felt, though. Drew's lips brushed her forehead, and she vaguely heard him whisper;

"Sleep, beautiful. You're quite safe here with us. Go to sleep."

Dana woke alone in a massive bed with her whole body still thrumming with pleasure. Stretching luxuriantly, hissing slightly as muscles unaccustomed to exercise protested their movement, she listened and heard male voices in the other room.

Her clothes were nowhere to be seen, so she shrugged and gathered a sheet around her, tucking it in toga-style before heading to the door.

What a sight greeted her eyes; Drew and Lex both wearing only loose shorts, moving around the kitchen in the early morning sunshine pouring through the big windows, making coffee and toast. They were both gleaming with a light sheen of sweat, had obviously been exercising. Leaning on the doorframe she just stared, lost for words.

Lex spotted her first, his smile broadening. "Good morning, Sleeping Beauty."

"Dana!" Drew exclaimed, smiling at her as well. "You're awake – we weren't sure what time you needed to get up for work…"

"I don't." Grinning back at him, she pushed off the doorframe, headed across the room and stole his coffee.

"You don't?" Drew parroted, bemused.

"I'm rostered off today. Mmm," Dana inhaled the coffee aroma, took a deep swig.

"Excellent," Lex said cheerfully, putting more bread into the toaster.

"It is?" Drew glanced across the top of her head at Lex.

"Yeah." Lex gave her a slow smile. "Means that after we've fed Dana some to get her energy levels back up, we can take her back to bed and spend the rest of the day makin' her scream our names."

Dana had to put the coffee down and hold onto the edge of the kitchen counter as her knees went weak at the mere suggestion. Drew grinned as he caught onto Lex's plan.

"I am *very* on board with that idea," he agreed. "How about you, beautiful?"

"Oh, yes *please*," she said fervently, then thought she'd sounded too eager – but both men were smiling broadly, obviously happy with her response.

"We could skip breakfast…" Drew began.

"No we can't," Lex disagreed. "We're *all* gonna need the energy."

"Fine, but I ain't waiting for you to cook up omelets or anything. Toast'll be fine."

Lex threw him a withering look before looking at Dana. "I can do eggs, if you'd like some…"

"Toast sounds good," she grinned, and Drew laughed.

"Great minds think alike. You can make yourself something fancy if you want, Lex, we'll just head on back to bed and start again without you."

"Fuck you," Lex snorted, reached to open the huge steel refrigerator cabinet. "Fine, you heathens. What do you like on your toast, Dana?"

She shrugged. "Whatever you have. I'm not fussy."

"Gourmet raspberry jam Drew picked up at a farmer's market?"

"Sounds awesome!" *Sounds a lot better than the Smuckers grape jelly I have at home*, Dana thought, smiling as Lex spread the toast thickly with the fruity spread and put it on a glossy white plate for her.

"Fresh juice?" Drew offered, and she glanced across to find him cutting up fruit to throw into a ridiculously expensive-looking juicer.

"Sure, why not." The morning was beginning to feel seriously surreal, as she sat down at the breakfast bar to eat her toast. She'd kept Drew's coffee, which Lex reached over to top off before pouring Drew another one.

A glass of pink-red juice was set down in front of her as she took her first bite of toast. Dana smiled up at Drew around it, had to swallow the toast hastily as he bent to kiss her. His tongue swept into her mouth, hand curling around the back of her neck to hold her still for him.

"Knock it off!" Lex whacked Drew none too gently on the shoulder. "Let the poor girl eat. I told you, she's gonna need the energy."

Drew actually pouted as he lifted his head, which made Dana giggle as she reached for her juice. "I'll be quick, promise."

"That's good, because I don't plan to be quick with you at all," Drew riposted, shoving at Lex. "And I'm eager to get started."

"You have no impulse control," Lex grumbled at him, though his eyes were laughing.

"That's why I keep you around." Drew grinned at him, and a little to Dana's surprise, the two men kissed, muscled arms sliding around each other to hold on closely.

She sat there with her mouth open, staring, until they parted and Lex grinned at her.

"You look a bit surprised there, angel. Did we shock you?"

Dana shook her head. "No, I figured you two had to have something going on. I just… didn't expect it to look quite so hot. Which is stupid, because you're both so fucking gorgeous. Really hot guy plus really hot guy apparently equals my panties melting off. If I was wearing any, that is," she glanced down at the sheet wrapped around her.

Drew groaned aloud, and Lex shook his head, chuckling. "You shouldn't have told us that, angel. Really. I'm having enough trouble restraining him as it is."

Giggling at their antics as Drew pretended to lunge for her and Lex gripped him around the waist, Dana hastily ate the rest of her toast, downing the coffee and juice. She'd no sooner licked the last crumb from her lips than Drew picked her bodily off the stool, almost ripped off the sheet and sat her down on the kitchen counter.

DANA'S DUO

"Lay back and relax, sweetness. I want some cream for *my* breakfast."

CHAPTER FOUR

Dana was vaguely aware of Lex's quiet laughter in the background, as he hastily swept away her plate and cup, said "Fuck, Drew, that was a cheesy line even for you!" but she couldn't bring herself to care, because Drew's hot tongue had delved straight into her pussy, his teeth scraping gently over her clit, making her shudder and groan out his name huskily.

"Oh, that's pretty, that's real pretty," Lex murmured from somewhere behind her. She heard him moving around, but didn't care what he was doing until she saw, through half-closed eyes, him move around to stand at the end of the kitchen counter beside her. His eyes fastened on Drew's blond head, shoved between Dana's thighs, thick slurping and humming noises letting Lex know just how much fun Drew was having down there. Dana was clearly enjoying herself too, writhing around on the counter and panting. Smiling at the pretty picture she made, Lex reached for her hands, gathered them together above her head and pinned both her wrists down with one strong hand.

Dana moaned as Lex restrained her hands. He smiled and leaned down to kiss her before his other hand moved stealthily to her breasts.

Dana squealed into Lex's mouth as he rubbed the piece of ice he was holding over one of her nipples. He chuckled roughly, nipping at her lips, moving his hand to the other breast to tease the ice over that nipple too, moving back and forth until both nipples stood up in stiff, aching peaks.

She could barely move, between Drew's strong hands on her hips and the way Lex had her hands pinned down. Instead she could only cry out as Lex continued kissing her and Drew's hot tongue worked its magic in her pussy, drawing her onwards and upwards to a climax as intense as it was inevitable. He stopped, though, just before she came, pulled back to look up at Lex, still playing with the nearly-melted chunk of ice on her nipples.

"Gimme that," Drew demanded thickly.

Lex chuckled darkly, handing the ice over. "Bet she'll make real pretty noises when you use that."

Dana whined, thrashing. The cold on her sensitive clit would be too much, she knew it… Drew popped the ice in his mouth and bent his head back to her pussy.

She screamed as Lex leaned down and sucked one chilled, throbbing nipple into his hot mouth at the same time as Drew's tongue pressed the ice chip on her clit. Two thick fingers pressed deep inside her, crooking upwards, Drew pushed the ice against her clit again, and Dana lost it completely, crying out hoarsely as she saw stars, the orgasm wracking her body in long, drawn-out tremors.

Drew groaned happily, slurping up Dana's juices, still working his fingers inside her even as her passage squeezed tightly down on them. Lifting his head finally, he looked up at Lex.

"You gotta fuck this beautiful pussy. She squeezes so tight, don't you, sweetheart?" His thumb rubbed over her clit, triggering a clench and another moan from Dana.

"Oh, I'm gonna," Lex let her nipple out of his mouth with a *pop*. "I'm gonna fuck her so hard she's seeing stars. You should try that glorious mouth. And that sweet, sweet ass."

"Decisions, decisions," Drew looked down at the beautiful girl spread out before them on the counter with a grin. "What to have first?"

Lex glanced around, smiled. "Over here." He lifted Dana easily into his arms, carried her over to their couch and settled down with her in his lap. "You okay, angel?" He stroked her hair lightly, twined a curl round his finger. "Need a break, or are you ready for more? Because I gotta tell you, I am absolutely desperate to get inside you."

She smiled up at him, shook her head. "I'm good. Better than good. Having you inside me sounds really nice right now." She could feel him hard against her hip through his thin shorts, ached to have him fill her. Glancing at the arm of the couch beside her, she smiled. "I have an idea, actually."

Drew had disappeared briefly; returned with a handful of foil packets. "That sounds dangerous," he arched a blond eyebrow at Dana as she hooked an arm around Lex's neck, pulled herself more upright. She smirked at him.

"You might think so. Come and stand here," she patted the arm of the couch. "And lose those shorts."

Grinning, Drew obeyed. "Getting bossy, are we?"

Dana smirked up at him as she knelt on the couch, putting her hands on the arm. "Do you like it when I'm bossy?" His cock was jutting out towards her, thick and proud. She breathed lightly over it, watched it twitch eagerly.

"Maybe," he allowed, reaching out to touch her face gently, smooth back her curly hair. "Such pretty hair," he murmured, and as Dana's lips parted, her tongue flickering out to lightly caress the tip of his cock, "such a gorgeous mouth, too."

"Such a gorgeous ass," Lex had been quiet behind her, but only because he was shedding his own shorts and rolling on a condom. His big hands smoothed over Dana's buttocks now, molding and squeezing. She shivered slightly, goosebumps springing up all down her spine.

"Does it like a little punishment, that pretty ass?" Drew asked, his fingers tightening in her hair. Dana looked up at him through her lashes and nodded, opening her mouth wider and leaning forward to take the thick crimson head of his cock into her mouth. "I thought it might. You should give her a little reprimand for trying to boss me around, Lex."

"Yeah?" Dana could hear the amusement in Lex's voice, though with the way Drew was holding her head, she couldn't look around to see him. "Trying to boss around the big boss, angel. That's very, very naughty."

"Mm-hm," she admitted, around a mouthful of cock. She even gave her ass a cheeky little wiggle.

The spank, when it landed, still took her by surprise. Squealing around her mouthful, Dana panted with excitement, adrenaline surging. Drew smiled down at her and firmed his grip on her hair, pulling her mouth a little further onto his cock. Wickedly, she laved her tongue along the underside, making Drew groan — and Lex spank her again, on the opposite cheek this time.

Dana's eyes almost rolled back in her head with pleasure. She quivered in place, unable to move, as Lex's long fingers trailed down her cleft.

"You like it, don't you?" Lex asked, leaning over her, his stubble rasping her soft skin as he kissed slowly up her spine. "Such a naughty, *wet* girl."

She moaned around Drew's cock, hollowing her cheeks and sucking on him as Lex suddenly thrust two fingers deep.

"Fuck," he muttered roughly, "fuck, *so* fucking wet."

"Go on, Lex," Drew said hoarsely. "Let her feel you while she blows me. Fuck her throat down on me."

Lex grunted, and withdrew his fingers, making Dana moan with the loss and try to wiggle her hips back towards him. A moment later he gave her what she really wanted, though, the thick, blunt head of his erection pressing against her, pushing her forward against Drew. She had to brace her arms to keep from being pushed too far; Drew, sensing her problem, let go of her hair and put his hands on her shoulders instead, helping to anchor her. Even so, she had to focus hard to suppress her gag reflex, concentrate on breathing through her nose as the head of his cock filled her throat.

"*Now* you're being a good girl," Drew murmured, praising her softly. Lex pulled back, eased forward again, his cock pushing an inch or so inside her as Drew held her head steady. They were perfectly in sync, Drew easing his hips back a little with every thrust of Lex's so that she didn't choke, until Lex was fully seated, deep inside her, filling her up. He held still then, frustrating Dana, who felt like she was about to explode; she wiggled her hips, trying to get him to move.

"When I'm ready, missy," Lex's hand smacked down on the meat of her outer thigh, making her shudder and moan in her throat, which in turn made Drew gasp, his fingers digging into her shoulders.

"Do that again," Drew ordered breathlessly, and Lex chuckled.

"Feel good?"

"Fuck yeah!"

"Let's make sure Dana's having a good time too, though, eh? She's a bit busy to tell us right now." His stubble rasped on her spine again as he bent over to press kisses on it slowly, and the hand which had been dealing punishment now crept around her and slid back between her thighs to scissor two fingers over her clit.

"Yep," Drew said as Dana moaned in her throat again, "that's good too. Fuck. *Fuuuuuck.*"

"That's what we're doing, in case you hadn't noticed," Lex sniped, but he sounded a little breathless too, as his hips began to rock slowly, his cock sliding in and out of Dana's sopping tunnel. His fingers nipped lightly at her clit, pushing back the hood and pressing on the sensitive nub, rubbing in a small tight circle.

Drew matched Lex's easy rhythm, cock sliding in and out of Dana's eager mouth as she sucked at him, eyes screwed shut, just savoring the sensations rippling through her. The build up towards climax was slower this time, Lex deliberately taking his time, bringing her up towards the edge and then backing off as the sounds she made around Drew became more frantic. There was absolutely nothing she could do to make him move faster, pinioned between them as she was. She just had to wait until Lex decided he was ready.

Or until Drew decided *he* was…

"Come on, buddy," Drew gritted out. "Come on, this feels too fuckin' good, I'm gonna come down Dana's throat any second."

Dana made a happy sound at the thought. Lex laughed hoarsely. "*Your* cock feels too fuckin' good? Look where mine is right now. Gonna fill you up good, angel," he rubbed faster over Dana's clit, his hips speeding up their rhythm. "You want that, eh? Filling up both ends at once?"

She couldn't answer, could only rotate her hips back into his thrusts and suck harder on Drew's cock as it slid in and out of her mouth, in and out, suddenly swelling thickly — she gasped and gulped greedily as hot seed suddenly jetted against the back of her throat, Drew groaning loudly as he came. Dana licked at him eagerly, but Lex seemed to take Drew's orgasm as a direction for him to fuck her more roughly and she had to stop, gasping for breath.

"Come on, sweetheart," Drew crouched down, reached under her to cup her breasts in his hands, roll her nipples firmly in his fingertips. "Come on, you can do it."

The room was filled with her cries, with Lex's uneven breathing as he accelerated again, pistoning roughly into her, skin slapping on skin almost obscenely loud. It felt wonderful; Dana's head dropped and she pressed her forehead on the arms of the couch between her braced hands, looking down along her body, at Drew's hands on her breasts, pinching and tweaking at her nipples. At Lex's hand still working between her thighs, rubbing hard at her clit. She couldn't see his cock sliding in and out of her — she'd need a mirror for that, and wasn't *that* a nice idea — but his balls hung thick and heavy, visible between her parted thighs, swinging and slapping against her ass with every stroke.

"I'm close," Dana sobbed, feeling the tingle beginning at the base of her spine, prickling all over her skin. Her whole body quivered as Lex slammed home again and again. "Please, oh god please, please don't stop."

"He ain't stopping, sweetheart," Drew assured her, plucking harder at her nipples, leaning in to give her a sloppy, messy kiss. "Not stopping until you come for us."

"Fuckin' right," Lex grated, lifting his hand off her hip to give her thigh a slap. "Come on, angel, come on *ohhh fucking hell!*"

Drew grinned with delight as Lex's blue eyes flew wide; his buddy had just found out the best possible way that Dana had a hell of a grip on her when she came. Their beautiful girl was nearly convulsing under Lex, strangled screams ripping from her throat, her eyes glazed over with ecstasy.

"*Fuuuuuck,*" there was no way that Lex could hold out; straining against Dana, he pumped himself dry, locked deep inside her quivering body, bent over her, holding her tightly against him. "Oh my God," he mumbled faintly after a moment, brow pressed to the curve of Dana's spine. "Wow. Okay. I didn't expect that. You got a grip like a boa constrictor, angel, what's with that?"

Cheek pressed on the arm of the couch, she smiled faintly, her eyes closed, as Drew smoothed her hair and Lex pressed slow kisses along her spine. "Yoga."

"God bless yoga," Lex said fervently, making her shake with laughter and him groan again as powerful internal muscles quivered around him. With a last sigh of pleasure, he put a hand on her ass and the other one at the base of his cock, pulling out slowly. "Amazing. You were right about that glorious pussy," he told Drew, collapsing to sit down.

"And you were right about that spectacular mouth," Drew answered, curling an arm around Dana and pulling her sit down down between them. "I'm looking forward to trying that ass out, too."

She groaned, heartfelt. "I really think I'm gonna need a bit of recovery time after that!"

"I'm pretty sure we all are," Drew chuckled, pressing a kiss to her brow. "Not now, sweetheart, I didn't mean now. Later."

"Mm," she hummed softly, relaxing into his embrace, leaning her head against his chest. He wasn't as built-up with muscle as Lex, not quite as bulky, but was still very nicely defined and solid. Gently, she poked a finger at his abs. "So this is what the great Drew Fischer hides under those perfectly tailored suits."

He chuckled, sounding pleased. Beside them, Lex huffed out a laugh as well, before getting up with a sigh. "Better visit the bathroom, but that looks like a nice cuddle pile," he pointed at the two of them. "Don't you move until I get back."

"Don't think I could move right now if I wanted to," Dana admitted against Drew's chest.

"You don't have to, sweetheart. It's quite all right." He smoothed her tangled curls gently, and she just lay against him, listening to the steady *thump-thump* of his heart until Lex came back.

"Definitely a nice cuddle pile," Lex twined himself around them from Dana's other side, nuzzling in to press kisses behind her ear until she giggled. "Mm mm. I like the filling in this sandwich," he murmured.

"You are ridiculous," she chuckled, turning her head towards him, which promptly led to him kissing her. Which led to Drew kissing her neck, not to be left out.

At that precise moment, a phone began to ring, somewhere in the kitchen. Drew stiffened, cursed under his breath.

"That's Alison's ring tone," Lex said. "You'd better get it."

"Yeah, yeah." Drew shoved himself to his feet, headed over to the counter and grabbed his phone. "Hi, Alison," he ran a hand through his blond hair distractedly as he spoke, looking back longingly at Lex and Dana still snuggling on the couch. "Yeah. Oh, right, Pochler came back to you on that deal? This morning?" Looking at the clock on the kitchen wall, he grimaced. "I could, yeah, I was planning to take the day, though… oh, dammit. All right. Tell him ten-thirty." Ending the call, he tossed the phone back onto the counter with a scowl. "I'm gonna have to go in to work."

"I should really go home and check out my apartment," Dana said with a small sigh, moving to push herself up. Lex's arms immediately tightened around her.

"I'll take you."

"Shouldn't you go with Drew?" she looked up at him.

"I'm Fischer, Inc.'s head of security, not Drew's bodyguard. He can look after himself." Lex looked amused. "I'll stay with you, Dana. I'll get one of my people to meet us at your place with your new keys."

"Okay," she conceded, realizing that she didn't have much choice about that. "Can I get a shower, first?"

"Of course you can," Lex smiled, leaning in to kiss her again before letting her go. "We won't have any clean clothes to fit you, but you can swipe one of Drew's business shirts if you like?"

"Sure," Drew was busy tapping in a text on his phone. He glanced up then, grinned. "Though I've just told Ross to meet me downstairs in twenty minutes. It's not much time. We'll have to share the shower."

Dana laughed as Lex hauled ass, scrambling to his feet and dragging her with him, hustling them both along in Drew's wake. About to protest that surely they wouldn't all fit, she shut her mouth on seeing the size of the shower. It was most certainly big enough for three; it was probably big enough for *six*, all tiled in glossy black marble with shining chrome fittings. Hot water rained down from huge shower roses as Drew touched a button.

"Holy wow," Dana said in awe, and Lex chuckled behind her.

"You like?"

"Hell, yes." She twisted her hair up into a hasty knot atop her head first, though, not wanting to get it soaked through now. It could wait until later for a wash.

Drew stepped into the water with a blissed-out sigh, stretching his arms above his head briefly. Dana stared in fascination at the shifting muscles in his back, even as Lex urged her under the hot streams as well.

Drew turned back to her, smiling, his hands slick with soap he'd just pumped from the glass and stainless steel dispenser on the wall. "Come here, you dirty, filthy girl. I'm gonna get you clean."

Dana gasped as his large hands curved around her sensitive breasts, laving them with the thick liquid soap. His fingers closed around the plump curves and he tugged gently, bringing her closer and bending his head to kiss her.

Lex hummed with pleasure at the sight of them both, pumped soap into his own hands and began to wash Dana's back, massaging the long muscles on either side of her spine, the tips of his long fingers pressing firmly until she moaned into Drew's mouth.

"Feel good?" Lex murmured hotly into Dana's ear, pressing himself against her back. He was half-hard again, rubbing his cock against the smooth curves of her ass. "You're so fucking sexy."

"God yeah," Drew agreed, lifting his head. "Wish we could stay here all day and just explore every glorious inch of you."

Lex's hand slid forward over one hip and down across her stomach, one knee nudging her thighs apart. "Guess we'll just have to settle for making sure that you'll want to come back around for seconds sometime, huh?"

Drew's soapy fingers tugged at her nipples, Lex's swirled over her clit, and Dana moaned wordlessly and sagged against Lex. He chuckled, nibbling lightly at her ear, his other arm wrapping around her ribs to hold her still while they tormented her, stimulating her erogenous zones.

"Don't think you have to worry about me not wanting a repeat performance," she gasped out as Lex's fingers slipped deeper into her cleft, pushing slowly up into her pussy, thumb working her clit now. Drew squeezed and massaged her nipples, Lex suckled a love bite slowly into her neck, and she slowly lost her mind yet again, shuddering out yet another climax, stars bursting behind her closed eyelids, her head falling back against Lex's muscled shoulder.

"That's it," Drew murmured as her mouth opened in a soundless scream. "Damn, yeah, beautiful, look at you, you're *spectacular*." He soaped his hands against and washed her down gently while Lex held her close. "I'm gonna have to go," Drew muttered finally, leaning in for one last kiss. "Take care of her?" he asked Lex, who nodded.

"You got it, buddy. See you later."

With a sigh, Dana pulled away from Lex as Drew left them. "We really should get moving. I'm sure you have loads of things to do as well…"

"Dana, I have absolutely nothing better to do than take care of you," Lex shook his dark head at her. "Don't for a moment think that I'm not more than happy to spend all day with you. Don't suppose I can convince you to come back to bed for a while?"

She laughed at that, shook her head a little bashfully, and Lex sighed theatrically. "Ah well. It was worth a shot."

Dana giggled at his silliness. It was charming, she reflected as he finally switched off the shower and handed her a large, fluffy towel, and very unexpected, to find that Lex Bradshaw, with his brooding, bad-boy air, could play the fool like that. He left her alone to dry off, popping back into the bathroom a couple of minutes later with her satchel, her discarded clothes from the previous evening and a crisp pinstriped cotton shirt.

"Reckon you'll look real cute in Drew's shirt," Lex winked at her before heading off again.

Smiling to herself, Dana put the shirt on. It was far too big, of course, but the fabric was beautiful quality. She folded the cuffs up above her elbows, tucked the tails into her slacks, and looked at herself in the mirror.

Not too bad at all for the morning after the wildest night of her life, she thought, with a grin at her reflection. Though she'd better do her best to at least cover up that stubble rash. She dug in her satchel for some makeup.

"You ready, Dana?" Lex called a couple minutes later.

"Just a minute!" she called back. "Are you calling a cab?"

"No, I'll drive."

DANA'S DUO

CHAPTER FIVE

Lex turned out to drive a smoke-colored Audi which looked inconspicuous at first glance. The engine's throaty roar told Dana that it was a much more powerful car than it looked, though. She settled back comfortably into the butter-soft leather of the passenger seat with a contented sigh, blinking with surprise when Lex leaned over to kiss her before starting the engine.

Back at her apartment building, Lex parked around the corner and took out his phone. A smiling young woman with a no-nonsense air about her met them at the front door and handed back Dana's keys, though there appeared to be a couple more of them than before. She fingered them and looked curiously at Lex.

"New door, new locks, new keys," he said laconically as they headed up to her small, top-floor studio apartment.

It was indeed a brand new door, with two brand new locks substantially more serious-looking than the single one that had been there before. Dana fiddled with the keys for a few minutes until she figured them out, finally letting them both into the apartment. She looked around silently. Lex moved up behind her, closing the door and putting his hands on Dana's shoulders gently.

"You're safe, Dana. He's not here."

She swallowed. "Everything... everything looks..."

"He slashed your bed and your couch with a knife, Dana." Lex didn't want to tell her the rest, but he had to; he couldn't let her figure it out for herself. "He had about twenty minutes here alone before I got here with the police."

Dana's arms wrapped around her stomach, clutching defensively at herself. Slowly, gently, Lex wrapped his arms around her. "My people got rid of everything he touched, Dana. I promise."

"Everything?" Her voice was quite small.

"When we came in, he was in your closet, cutting up your clothes."

"Oh, you've got to be kidding me!" Her instinctive fear was subsumed by rage as she pulled away from him and headed for her closet. Throwing open the door, she swore loudly as she found it three-quarters empty, only a few things still hanging there. Spinning back around, she stared at Lex. "What else?"

Ruefully, he gestured to the small set of drawers beside her bed.

"Oh, no." Dana yanked the top drawer open to find it completely empty. The second one, too. The third. "What the hell?"

"You don't want to know what he did to your underwear, Dana. You really don't," Lex shook his head. "Drew's secretary Alison is getting you a credit card; you can replace everything. Get all new stuff."

Slamming the drawers shut, Dana shook her head, biting on her lower lip. Tears of frustration welled in her eyes as she looked around.

"It's *all* contaminated. I don't — I don't want *anything* here."

"Okay," Lex said quietly, keeping his voice steady and even. "I don't think you should stay here. Come home with me, at least another night until you decide what to do. We've got a spare room, if that's what you want."

She took a deep breath, nodded jerkily, and when Lex held out his arms to her, she ran into them and pressed her face against his chest.

"You're sure there's nothing you want here? Nothing personal, photos, books…"

Dana shook her head against his chest. "Everything like that's stored in my personal online cloud. Can't be lost that way."

"Modern girl, how sensible you are." He kissed her forehead gently, hugging her close. "You want to go?"

"Yes, please."

He took the keys from her hand gently, locked the door behind them. They were on their way downstairs when his phone rang in his pocket. Lex pulled it out, preparing to reject the call when he saw the caller ID and cursed. "Damn, it's the police detective in charge of the case. I'd better take it, Dana."

She shrugged and nodded her agreement. Lex answered the call with a clipped "Lex Bradshaw speaking," and talked to the detective on the other end for a few moments, asking for an update.

"Yes," he said then, "she's with me now, actually. No, not at the precinct, she's a *victim*, not a suspect. No, not at her apartment either. Come to my office, you can talk to her there." He raised his eyebrows at Dana questioningly; she shrugged and nodded. The police would want to take a statement from her, she supposed, and Lex was right; she didn't want to go down to the precinct or wait in her sullied apartment for them. The thought of Lex being with her during the interview was immensely comforting too, and she said as much when he hung up the phone after agreeing to meet the detective at his office in an hour.

"Of course I'll stay with you," he said almost fiercely, taking her hand in his. "Of *course*. But first, let's go get you a few new things to wear."

That made her smile. "It could wait…"

"No, I'm damned if that asshole's gonna leave you with just one outfit. No way. Let's hit the shops, angel."

Dana had to laugh, but Lex was insistent. Not only that, but he insisted on taking her to Macy's and buying her not one but half a dozen new outfits, lingerie — which he laughingly suggested that she should model for him and Drew later — and four new pairs of shoes. He bought her lunch at a sushi bar too before taking her back to Fischer, Inc. to meet with the detective. They got there with just a couple of minutes to spare so she didn't have time to change, but Lex suggested that she could at least freshen up in the private bathroom off his office.

The case detective was already in the office with Lex when Dana emerged, smoothing her hair. A tall, attractive Black woman in her mid-thirties, Dana guessed, she turned to give Dana a warm smile.

"Ms. Moretti. Hello, I'm Detective Janet Kenton, and this is my partner Detective Natalie Moore."

The other woman was standing a little off to one side. A willowy blonde, she ran her eyes over Dana with a faintly incredulous expression and didn't offer her hand to shake.

Lex moved closer to Dana, guided her gently to sit at the table over to one side of his office, where four chairs waited.

"Do you mind if we record this interview?" Kenton asked politely, setting a recorder down on the table.

"Not at all, as long as you don't mind if I do too," Lex replied. Kenton blinked, but nodded without comment.

"Now, Ms. Moretti — may I call you Dana?" she asked with a friendly smile.

"Please do."

"Good. Now, I've already been over the report you filed with Lex yesterday. But is there anything else you can tell us about what might have made Graham Harding snap and go to your apartment last night?"

"He did get fired," Dana said with a shrug. "I suppose it's not exactly a stretch for him to twist it around in his head and make it somehow my fault instead of his."

Kenton nodded, scribbled something in her notebook. Natalie Moore leaned forward.

"You seriously expect us to believe that with no encouragement from you at all, Harding developed such a violent obsession with you that he went and wrecked your apartment, ejaculated all over your underwear and wrote WHORE on your bathroom mirror in your lipstick?" Her tone was frankly incredulous.

Dana flinched back at hearing exactly what had happened in her apartment. Lex's hand found hers under the table, his warm fingers wrapping firmly around hers in a supportive gesture that enabled her to answer.

"Yes," she said, fighting to keep her voice steady. "I do expect you to believe that, because it's the truth."

"You weren't involved with him romantically in any way?" Moore pressed.

"No, I was not."

"Because he claims that you were. He claims that you were having an affair and that this is all a lovers' tiff."

"What?" Dana's jaw dropped.

Kenton sighed, gestured to Moore to be quiet. "That's correct, Dana. Harding and his wife are separated, in the process of getting a divorce. Harding claims that you and he started having an affair when you joined Fischer, Inc. some… eight months ago?" she checked back a page in her notebook. "His wife filed for divorce *six* months ago, and Harding claims it was because she found out about the two of you. He left his wife for you, and when he found out you were cheating on him he went to your apartment. When he found out you weren't there he assumed you were with your new lover, and he damaged your things in a fit of rage."

Dana was so incredulous she couldn't think of a thing to say. She just sat with her mouth hanging open in astonishment.

"I've never heard such a steaming pile of bullshit in my life," Lex said crisply.

Both detectives blinked, looked away from Dana. "How so, Lex?" Moore said, and her tone was soft and honeyed, decidedly flirtatious.

"I personally witnessed Harding harassing Dana physically and pestering her to go out with him yesterday."

"Go out with him, or go out with him *again?*" Moore persisted.

Dana had heard quite enough. Pulling out her phone, she put it down on the table and slid it over to Moore.

"What's this?" the blonde gave her an unfriendly look.

"Evidence. If Graham Harding claims we've been having an affair for eight months, there has to be some, right? I must have called him, texted him, emailed him. Otherwise, how did his wife find out? Have you *talked* to his wife, by the way? Asked *her* why she left him? Because I can tell you for damn sure it's not because I was having an affair with him."

"Felicity Harding is out of town," Kenton said, "we're waiting for her to get back in order to interview her."

"And in the meantime, Graham Harding is trying to talk his way out of a jail cell by weaving a web of lies to make you think he's a victim," Lex said angrily. "Or have you forgotten already, Janet, that you've got a bandage on your left arm from where he stabbed you with that knife before I knocked him out?"

Kenton shifted a little uncomfortably in her chair. "I haven't forgotten. And he won't get bail until that charge, at least, is dealt with."

"But you're not going to charge him with breaking into my apartment and trashing my stuff because he's somehow convinced you that *I'm* the bad person in all of this?" Dana said incredulously. "That I'm the home-wrecker who tempted a man away from his wife, drove him mad with lust and then had an affair with someone else, so he cracked?"

Kenton looked even more uncomfortable. "Right now, it *is* your word against his," she said.

"… the word of someone who hasn't done anything wrong against the word of a lunatic who broke into a locked apartment and wrecked the place before stabbing a police officer?"

Lex laughed and made absolutely no effort to turn it into a cough. "She's got you there."

Moore looked affronted, but Kenton nodded. "It's a good point. The restraining order your attorneys filed this morning has been granted, by the way," she added to Lex. "Though it's a moot point since Harding is in a cell. We'll be back in touch when we've talked to Felicity Harding," she told Dana, closing her notebook and picking up her tape recorder to switch it off.

Moore said nothing, but her gaze was openly scornful as she raked it over Dana before turning to farewell Lex in sugary sweet tones, holding onto his hand much too long.

Lex walked the two police officers to the elevator before returning to find Dana in tears.

"Oh, angel," closing his office door, he closed the space between them quickly, pulling her into his arms. "Don't be upset. Please. None of this was your fault."

"I know," she choked, hands fisting in his shirt. "I know that. They just — they — I felt like they didn't believe me. That they didn't think I was attractive enough to inspire someone to behave like that…"

"I call bullshit on that," Lex said fiercely. "You inspire *me* to want to kill that asshole Harding for scaring you and putting you through this, and I promise you Drew feels the same. You're beautiful, Dana, you're passionate and smart and incredibly desirable."

"I am?" She looked up at him with tears streaking her cheeks, her lips puffy and trembling.

"Yes, dammit!" Bending his head to kiss her, he ground his groin against hers deliberately, grinning against her lips when she gasped, feeling the thick hardness he was pressing against her through their clothes. "See what you do to me? I could get pretty obsessed with you too, I confess."

Dana licked her lips. "I don't think I'd mind if it was you," she whispered.

"No?" His blue eyes gleamed down at her, and then slowly, he slid down to his knees, hooking his fingers into the waistband of her slacks. "Let me show you just how desirable I think you are," he murmured.

Dana was very far from objecting, as Lex tugged down her slacks and panties, encouraged her to step out of them with her shoes, before nuzzling up her thighs. He pushed her back gently until her shoulders hit the wall — at the same time as his tongue flicked over her clit.

"Oh jeez, Lex," she whimpered, fingers sliding into his dark hair. "Someone could come in."

"They won't," he took his mouth from her just long enough to say. "Put your leg over my shoulder." He reached up to unbutton the borrowed pinstripe shirt she was still wearing, gazing up at her breasts confined by sheer lace, heaving as she breathed quickly.

Dana moaned, lifting one leg as directed to put it over Lex's shoulder, opening the angle for him to get more of his mouth onto her pussy. She felt briefly unbalanced, but his strong hands curled around her thighs, steadying and holding her still as his tongue swept slowly from back to front, slurping moisture from her entrance up to her clit.

Lex hummed with pleasure, enjoying the taste of Dana's juices as she sagged in his grip, her hands messing up his hair as she held on tight, not that he gave a damn about that. She was more than clearly enjoying herself, soft throaty moans sounding out as he worked her clit with his tongue, swirling his tongue over it lightly at first, then in firmer licks until she was almost yelling his name, and he closed his lips and suckled. She was getting close, he could tell from the way her fingers clenched in his hair, her juices flooding his mouth.

"Please," Dana sobbed, "please, Lex…"

He took his mouth off her and grinned up at her, her slick shining wetly on his lips and chin.

"Oh god don't stop, you're so mean!"

Lex chuckled, scrambling to his feet and unbuckling his belt. "I want to feel you come around me, angel. Love feeling you come apart." He reached in his pocket for his wallet.

"Don't — don't need it," Dana batted the foil packet away as he extracted it from his wallet. "Got an implant, you can't get me pregnant, and I'm clean. It's been quite a while since I had sex — before last night, anyway."

"Drew and I have been pretty exclusive for years," Lex admitted. "You trust me that much?"

"Please, Lex, I want to feel you. All of you." She looked up at him with pure trust in her pretty brown eyes, and Lex groaned under his breath. The thought of sheathing his aching, throbbing cock deep inside Dana's wet, gripping cavern without that thin latex barrier between them deadening the sensation made him even more frantic to get inside her. Discarding the packet and his wallet, letting his pants and shorts fall to his ankles, he lifted Dana up easily with both hands under her ass and pinned her back against the wall of his office.

"Put your legs around me," he grated out. "I'm gonna fuck you right here, right up against this wall."

"Oh god, yes please," Dana gasped, moaning with delight as he lowered her slowly onto his rigid, straining cock. "Oh, *Lex*."

"I like the way you say my name," he sought her lips with his own as her arms wound around his neck, holding on tight, her heels digging into his ass. "*Fuck*, yeah," as he sank deep into her hot, welcoming core. "Damn, Dana, that's good, that's so *fucking* good."

She could only whimper against his searching, seeking mouth as his hips began to rock, slowly at first but soon snapping back and forwards hard and fast, slamming into her roughly, his powerful hands on her hips holding her at the perfect angle for his cock to chafe over her clit with every rough stroke.

Dana spared a moment to hope that the office walls were soundproof. Though Lex's mouth was absorbing the loudest of the cries and moans she couldn't quite suppress, they were making a fair bit of noise, even more as the heat simmering in her core approached full boil again.

"Yes," she sobbed, her nails digging into his shoulders through his shirt. "Lex, please, please, *yesssss*," as he surged against her, snarling out her name triumphantly, heat blasting inside her as her internal muscles spasmed, clamping down on his spurting, jetting cock.

Lex's fingers dug into the soft flesh of her ass hard; he'd leave the marks of his fingerprints on her skin, not that either of them cared. Clinging to his broad shoulders, Dana moaned out his name again and again as the waves of climax rolled through her, tingling up and down her spine.

"So good," Lex muttered against her hair, "so fucking good, Dana, *damn*." The last word was a long, drawn-out sigh, before he carefully lifted her off him and set her down on shaking legs. She leaned back against the wall, breathing hard, waiting for the hammering of her pulse to slow. She could feel Lex's seed trickling out of her, sticky on her thighs, knew she should head for the bathroom to clean up. Right then, though, she didn't want to move at all, not with Lex's arms still close about her, her head tucked into the strong curve of his neck.

"Thank you," she murmured at last.

"Thank *me*, for what?" Lex pulled back to look at her face.

"For being exactly what I needed." Reaching up to kiss him again, she grinned at his slightly bemused expression before slipping out of his grasp and heading to the bathroom, leaving him to straighten his clothes and pick hers up off the floor.

DANA'S DUO

CHAPTER SIX

Coming back out of the bathroom wearing only Drew's shirt, now buttoned back up, Dana smiled in thanks as Lex handed her the rest of her clothes. She was just putting her shoes back on when his phone rang.

"Bradshaw," he answered it curtly, frowning and looking at his watch a few moments later. "Can it wait?" He sighed impatiently when the person on the other end obviously answered in the negative. "Fine. I'll be down shortly." Hanging up, he turned to Dana. "Angel, I'm so sorry, something's come up…"

She reached up to put a fingertip against his lips, quieting him. "Lex. Don't worry about it. I work here, remember? I'll just run down to my desk and do a few odd jobs. Come find me when you're finished."

Lex smiled at that before gathering his in his arms. "Not letting you out of my sight without one last kiss," he said, and proceeded to kiss her so thoroughly she was gasping for breath and had to hold onto his desk to keep herself upright when he finally let go. Giving her a wicked grin over his shoulder, Lex left her alone to regain her composure.

Which took quite a few minutes, another trip to the bathroom to repair her makeup yet again, and a cold bottle of water she swiped from the small fridge in his office. Finally, cooled off a little bit, Dana let herself out and headed down to her regular workstation.

"You're not rostered on today," was the first thing her boss said when she walked in the door. The office was almost empty, everyone obviously out on calls.

"So pretend I'm not really here," Dana riposted with a grin. "Won't be for long, I hope."

"All right, but we're busy, make yourself useful," she was told.

She settled at her desk, checking her email and attending to a few small issues that had cropped up. The phone on her desk rang after about fifteen minutes and she frowned at it in annoyance. "I'm not really here, Shaun!" she leaned to the side and called along the office.

"Pick it up!" he yelled back.

She sighed and scooped up the handset. "What?"

"Special request for you. The big boss has apparently stuffed something on his computer and he wants you up there."

"The big boss…?"

"Mr Fischer himself, Dana, so get your ass in gear!"

She hung up the phone before she started laughing, grabbed up her satchel. "On it, boss!" she waved a sketchy salute at Shaun as she hurried past on the way to the elevators.

Alison, Drew's secretary, smiled at Dana when she arrived at the office. "Go right on in, Ms. Moretti. Before you do, I have your new card here, though?" She held out an envelope.

"New card?" Dana's brow furrowed as she took the envelope.

"Credit card. Mr Fischer requested that I get you one, in order for you to replace your things which were wrecked."

Dana wasn't quite sure how to feel about that, but Alison wasn't the right person to take it up with, so she just murmured a quiet thank you and knocked lightly on Drew's office door.

"Come in," he called, and she obeyed, closing the door behind her. Drew stood up from behind his desk and smiled when he saw her, the smile widening when he noticed that she was wearing his shirt.

"Oh, sweetheart, do you *ever* look good in my shirt." He eyed her admiringly, coming around the desk towards her. "Love it. Lex told me he got you some new stuff but I bet it doesn't look half as good on you as that does."

"About that," Dana waved the envelope Alison had given her at him. "I can replace my own things, Drew. The insurance will pay for what got trashed, once I make a claim."

He eyed her thoughtfully. "This isn't some attempt to buy you, or your affections, Dana," he said finally. "I'd do the same thing for any of my employees."

"Even so." She put the envelope down on his desk. "Thanks, but no thanks."

"But you'll keep the things Lex bought you." Drew looked almost jealous.

"Because right now, I have nothing to wear otherwise unless I raid all the shirts out of your wardrobe," Dana sniped back teasingly, smiling.

"You'd soon be cursing me out when you had nothing to wear."

That made Drew chuckle; he held out his arms to her and she went into them willingly, putting her arms around his lean waist and hugging on tight. He stroked her back gently, soothingly, making no attempt to break the embrace.

"Lex told me the police were a bit tough on you," Drew said quietly against her hair a little while later. "He called me, a few minutes ago," when Dana looked up at him questioningly. "He's been delayed. He'll come up here when he's done and we can all leave together, but I didn't want you getting stuck with working this afternoon, not when it's supposed to be your day off."

"There's nothing wrong with your computer at all, is there?" Dana said with a grin. She'd already surmised as much; had it confirmed when Drew nodded.

"Just didn't want you to have to work, not after that. Why don't you have a rest?" He nodded towards a comfortable-looking couch at one side of the office.

She *was* feeling tired. It had been a long and exhausting night, not to mention a roller-coaster ride of tumultuous emotions from the moment Harding had accosted her outside the server room the day before. *Was it only yesterday?* Dana wondered as Drew guided her gently towards the couch. Lying down, she smiled as he covered her with a blanket.

"This your crash spot, sometimes?"

"Only when Lex and I have had a fight," Drew said with a rueful grin. "Even then he usually turns up to drag me back home."

"Lex said you guys had been together — exclusive — for a long time," that remark had been eating away at Dana for the last little while. "Why me, then?"

Drew smiled at that. "Because we do both like women, and frankly, because you're the first woman in a long time to tempt *both* of us." The tip of one long finger traced delicately over her lower lip, his blue-green eyes fixed on hers. "You're very tempting, Dana."

Drew's voice had dropped to a husky rasp. Dana stared up at him, licked her lips; Drew groaned and laughed, leaning down to kiss her.

"Don't look at me like that or I won't get any more work done this afternoon either!"

She smiled, turning on her side as he moved away, back over to his desk. Drew was so sweet; although she sensed he could be just as hard as Lex, he hid it under that handsome, preppy exterior most of the time. Watching him sit down and reach out to pull his laptop back in front of him, she closed her eyes and tried to sleep.

Of course, despite feeling really quite exhausted, sleep was nowhere near her. Especially not with her mind insistent on replaying the way Drew had looked at her when he ran his finger over her lips and said how tempting she was. She cracked her eyelids open a fraction to peek at him. He had his back to her right now, swiveled around on his chair talking quietly on the phone, looking out at the view.

Suddenly struck by a wicked idea, she slipped quietly off the couch and crawled quickly under Drew's desk. He swiveled back to it at that moment, reaching for his laptop to pull up a memo he was talking about to the person on the other end of the call, and Dana took her opportunity.

Drew had to stifle a gasp as his fly suddenly slid down, deft little fingers reaching to unbuckle his belt. Dana peeked mischievously up at him from under the desk and he shook his head at her. She grinned wickedly and edged forward to kneel between his feet.

"You there, Fischer?" a voice barked in his ear.

"Yes, still here," Drew replied, watching in almost hypnotized fascination as Dana edged his cock out of his shorts and leaned in, little pink tongue coming out to flick lightly at the tip. He was hardening quickly, knew he wouldn't be able to remain coherent for much longer as her mouth opened wide and she took him straight down deep. Biting down on the moan that threatened to erupt, he said breathlessly, "Something's come up. I'll have to give you a call back tomorrow, Paul," and ended the call before the other man could even object.

"Something is definitely *up*," Dana said, letting him out of her mouth for a moment before diving back down on it. Hollowing her cheeks, she sucked on his cock like it was her favorite lollipop.

"You wicked little madam," Drew groaned as her slender fingers crept in to join the play, working down to curl around his balls, rolling them, teasing them. Dana gave him wide, innocent eyes; entirely incongruous with the obscene picture her lips made stretched wide around his cock. "Oh no. I can feel what you're doing with your tongue, don't you dare try and look innocent. Didn't Lex and I give you a lesson last night in what bad girls get?"

Dana couldn't suppress the moan in her throat at the memory, and Drew grinned, putting his hand in her hair and gently but remorselessly tugging her upwards until she had to let his cock out of her mouth, let herself be pulled up to straddle his lap.

"Bad girls get thoroughly fucked," Drew told her, letting go of her hair and reaching for the buttons of her shirt. "They might even get their bottoms spanked, if they're bad enough." He smiled as the shirt parted to reveal her bra, pushed it back off her shoulders to catch her arms behind her and leaned down to kiss and nip at the soft flesh welling smoothly above the bra cups. "Hmm?"

"Huh?" Dana said, not understanding the question he seemed to be asking.

"Are you naughty enough to need your bottom spanking?" Drew plucked at her bra until her nipple sprang free over the lacy cup, suckled it into his mouth. His other hand worked down in between them to unfasten her slacks, push inside to rub over her panties. "You smell like Lex," he murmured against her breast, inhaling deeply, "like Lex, and fucking. He had you again, didn't he?"

"Y-yes," Dana admitted breathlessly, "in his office."

"That why you decided to behave so badly in mine?" A long finger flicked the crotch of her panties aside, grazed over her clit. "Or did you just want to see how far you could push me? I shan't ignore you again, I promise."

"G-good," she panted, as his finger sank up to the knuckle in her pussy. "I — I like having your attention."

"Oh, sweetheart, you're going to get my *full* attention," Drew promised darkly, just before lifting her off his lap and his finger in one smooth movement. Dana cried out with loss, but Drew only chuckled, rising swiftly to his feet and turning her around, pushing her to bend over the desk, tugging the shirt further down her arms and giving it a deft twist around her wrists to trap them together. Startled, she wiggled, but he pinned her down with a strong hand at the small of her back, the other tugging her slacks and panties down and stripping them off along with her shoes.

Dana looked back over her shoulder at Drew, saw him slowly, deliberately pulling his tie loose. Unbuttoning his shirt. Wide-eyed, she stared as he stripped off unhurriedly.

"Naughty girl," Drew smoothed his palm over her buttock slowly. "You're a very, very naughty girl, aren't you, Dana? Letting Lex fuck you in his office, crawling under my desk to suck my dick. Such a bad, bad girl."

She could feel her pussy bubbling with excitement. "Yes," she whimpered, and Drew smiled and smacked her right buttock firmly.

Knowing Alison was sitting right outside the door, Dana tried to bite down on her squeal. She went up on her tiptoes, pushing her breasts hard down on the desk, shoving her ass up towards Drew.

"Please," she gasped out breathily.

"Let me see," Drew's big hand stroked lightly over the red hand print he'd just left. "That one was for stealing my shirt."

"You said I could!"

He spanked her again. "That's for cheeking me."

She squeaked with indignation, but her feet were already shifting further apart. "What else?" she whispered, through a throat tight with excitement.

"Hmm, well there's definitely at least one for fucking Lex when I wasn't even there to watch," he spanked her left cheek, this time.

"He ate me out, too," Dana admitted.

"And one for that." Drew chuckled quietly as Dana presented reason after reason he should punish her more, punish her until her beautifully rounded ass was cherry-red from the spanking and she was moaning continuously, her hips rocking against the desk as she sought desperately for the friction she craved.

"I let him fuck me without a condom," Dana gasped out finally.

Drew froze, surprised. "You did?"

"Yes," she peeked at him over her shoulder. "I've got an implant, and I'm clean. That's when he told me you two were exclusive."

"The operative word there, sweetheart, is 'were'," Drew said quietly. "I'm not gonna spank you for that. I bet Lex fucking loved it."

"I'd like you to do that too," Dana told him, and he groaned.

"*Such* a naughty girl."

Bent over his desk this way, his cock was literally only a few inches from where he knew they both desperately wanted it to be. Moving to place his feet between hers, he reached beneath her to grasp her breasts, pluck at her nipples. "You want this? Want a good fucking on the boss's desk, naughty girl?"

"Yes," Dana could only pant as Drew's thick cock began to push into her, the way eased by how very, very wet the spanking he'd just dealt out had made her. She writhed desperately, trying to get him in deeper, faster; he only chuckled and pinched her nipples harder, moving at his own, tortuously slow pace.

"Greedy little madam. Take it easy. No rush."

It was at that very moment that the door opened.

Shocked, Dana bit off a scream when she saw Lex standing there. He took in the sight before him with one comprehensive glance and grinned, shutting the door quickly behind him.

"Well, well. What do we have here? Thought you were gonna let her have a nap, Drew?"

Drew grinned at Lex over Dana's prone body. "That was the plan, until a certain little madam decided to crawl under my desk and attempt to blow me when I was on the phone."

"Oho!" Lex looked at Dana, trapped face-down on the desk, her ass scarlet from Drew's spanking, his cock shoved deep into her pussy. "You don't have to tell me the rest. I think I can figure it out."

Dana wiggled hopefully. Drew wasn't moving, and she needed friction quite desperately. He smacked her bottom again almost casually, making her jump and squeal.

"Go on," Lex said, coming over to the other side of the desk. "Give her a good fucking for being such a naughty girl, Drew."

"Got a better idea," Drew pulled out, making Dana cry out with loss. "I still didn't get to fuck that gorgeous ass." His fingers delved between her thighs. "She's plenty wet." He rubbed slick up over her hole, making Dana shudder with sudden need as one finger pressed into the tight ring of muscle. "What do you think, sweetheart, think you can take both of us again?"

"Yes," she panted, "yes, please, I want it." Heat was spreading inside her at the very thought, the memory of how they'd both felt moving inside her the previous night making her feel shaky with wanting it again. "Please, I want you both, want both those big cocks in me," she looked up at Lex pleadingly, her eyes wide.

"*Greedy* little girl," Drew pushed another slick-soaked finger into her ass to join the first. "What do you think, Lex, shall we give her what she wants?"

Lex was already stripping off his shirt. "Well, since I'm gonna get what I want too, I'm inclined to, yeah."

"Again," Drew said pointedly.

"Oh, don't sulk just because you weren't there to watch. You spanked her bottom while *I* wasn't here to watch, so let's call it even."

Drew chuckled at that. His fingers had never stopped working in Dana's ass, scissoring her open. It felt amazing, the slight burn adding to the spiral of sensations already going on inside her; she was barely aware of their joking conversation above her while Lex removed his clothes.

She was the only one wearing anything, she realized when Drew finally slid his fingers out of her and picked her up off his desk, carrying her over to the couch where Lex reclined comfortably, a broad grin on his face. The grin wasn't the only thing ready and welcoming about him; he was stroking his cock to full arousal, watching as Drew just set Dana down on top of him before reaching to untangle and remove the shirt caught on her arms, unclasping her bra and removing that too.

"That's it, these poor babies have been a bit neglected, haven't they?" Lex released his erection as Drew set Dana neatly down on it, reached up to take her breasts in his hands. She moaned as he sank deep into her, strong fingers tugging and tweaking at her nipples. "Damn, so pretty," Lex murmured, watching as she took him inside.

Drew had taken hold of her wrists, was holding her hands behind her back so her breasts jutted out towards Lex.

"Gorgeous, isn't she?" Drew said hoarsely. "We're gonna have to film her."

Lex groaned, hips jerking sharply upwards. Dana gasped as he hit right on the most sensitive spot inside her.

"You like that idea?" Drew muttered in her ear as he shifted into position behind her. "Maybe we'll film with you blindfolded. So you'll only get to see it later. Tie you up to watch it. I bet by the end you'd be absolutely desperate to get off."

She was desperate to get off *now*. Drew's suggestion only made it worse. "Mirror," Dana panted as the tip of his cock nudged at her ass. "Was thinking — we need a big mirror."

"Yeah," Lex agreed, his voice harsh with strain. "That's good. Like that idea."

"Naughty girl, making wicked suggestions like that," Drew bit at her shoulder as he pushed a little deeper. "We like bad girls, don't we, Lex?"

"Best kind," Lex agreed deeply, his hips rolling gently, keeping the pleasure thrumming through Dana as Drew stretched her uncomfortably. She was starting to feel very full now. Lex's fingers plucked at her nipples constantly, Drew let go of her wrists at last and reached around to find her clit, tapping on it in a quick, irregular pattern that made her shudder.

"Yes," Dana gasped, feeling the tension ratcheting up inside her suddenly, drawing her up like clockwork wound tight, until she felt as though she might snap. "Oh god, yes, so close, *please*," her limbs were shaking, every inch of her skin tingling as Drew finally seated himself fully inside her.

"Come on, then," Drew growled. "Come on, I want to feel it. We're gonna fuck you through it…" his hips snapped back and forth hard, once, twice, three times as his fingers strummed on her clit, and Dana lost it completely. Drew put his free hand over her mouth quickly to muffle the screams she let out, grinning over her shoulder at Lex, who was laughing silently. Dana made very nice sounds but she was noisy, and they weren't entirely sure how soundproof the office was. Alison no doubt had a pretty fair idea of what they were up to anyway and she was utterly discreet, but anyone else who happened to pass might be curious.

"Fucking gorgeous," Lex muttered, dropping his hands from Dana's breasts to grasp her hips. "So tight, angel."

"Yeah," Drew had to drop his forehead against Dana's neck for a moment, breathe deeply as her tight internal muscles sucked at both of them. "Wow. You weren't kidding about how good her ass is."

"Mm," Lex was contending with his own problems right then. Finally Dana's muscles slacked off, though, and he was able to take a deep breath. "You having a good time, angel?" he checked as she still shivered and gasped.

She couldn't speak, could only nod blindly as Lex's hips began to shift again, his cock sliding smoothly inside her soaked, still-clenching tunnel. Drew matched his rhythm, synchronizing perfectly, only pulling out when Lex was pushing in so they were never both filling her at the same time. Drew's fingers kept on playing over her clit, sliding all over the already wildly sensitive little organ. He kept his other hand over her mouth, ready to muffle any more loud noises she let out, letting Lex control their pace with his grasp on her hips.

Dana was utterly helpless to do anything but let them use her as they wished, strong bodies shifting against hers, thick cocks shuttling in and out of her dripping holes as they both took their pleasure, coaxing more from her at the same time. She wasn't even sure she *could* come again, her body wrung out from the pleasure they'd given her in the last few hours, but they seemed quite determined to prove her wrong.

"Come on, angel," Lex exhorted her, watching the strain on her face. "You can do it."

She felt so *open* as they both fucked in and out of her. Utterly vulnerable in a way she'd never felt before, and yet completely safe, held in two pairs of strong arms, both men clearly determined to see to her pleasure just as much as her own. Drew suckled on her neck, giving her a matching hickey to the one Lex had put on her earlier, his fingers never ceasing their play on her clit as the friction inside her once again built to an unbearable level.

This time, the climax was so intense she almost blacked out. She was distantly aware of Lex and Drew groaning and cursing in low, harsh voices as she clamped down on them, squealing her ecstasy against Drew's muffling hand before collapsing in a near-faint on Lex's chest. Overwhelmed by their own orgasms, it took a minute or so for the men to realize that she was overcome.

"Dana. Dana!" Lex shook her shoulders gently as Drew swore and eased out of her.

"Ummm," she mumbled faintly against Lex's neck.

"Get her some water," Lex told Drew, carefully easing Dana off him and laying her back on the couch. She made grumpy noises and clutched at him, so he held onto her while Drew fetched her some water.

"You okay, angel?" Lex asked, holding the glass for her to sip.

"Nope," Dana mumbled, eyes closed. "You killed me. With sex."

Lex grinned with relief at her words. "I think we just wore you out, angel." Drew arrived back then with a damp towel from the bathroom to clean her up; she grumbled again as Lex shifted her around.

"Think we'd best get you home, huh?" Lex kissed her brow, smoothed her tangled curls.

"Don't wanna go home," she mumbled into his shoulder. "Wanna stay with you an' Drew."

He paused, arrested, hand still on her hair. "That's what I meant, angel. Home with us. Our home."

Drew was quietly pulling on his clothes. "I'll order in some dinner," he suggested to Lex, who nodded.

"Good plan. Come on, angel, we gotta get your clothes back on."

CHAPTER SEVEN

By the time they arrived back at the apartment, dinner had been delivered, a delicious-smelling assortment of Chinese food. Absolutely starving, Dana dived in and started opening cartons.

"Yum, spring rolls," she stuffed one into her mouth, grinned around it at Lex when he chuckled at her and reached to open more cartons.

"Good thing you always tend to over-order, I think Dana's worked up an appetite," he said laughingly to Drew.

"She'll need the energy," Drew pointed out, grabbing a spring roll for himself before Dana ate them all. "Think I do too, that said."

Lex smirked, grabbing some plates and serving himself a heaping portion of fried rice. "You're spending too much time behind that desk, Drew. Getting soft."

Dana snorted, swallowing her last bit of spring roll. "Ain't much soft about either of you, I can tell you. Not from what I can feel."

That made them both laugh. Lex's phone rang just then, and he frowned, but answered it, going out into the other room to take the call. He was smiling when he returned.

"That was Detective Kenton, Dana. They've found Harding's wife. She and her children were in hiding in a battered women's shelter; a friend let her know Harding had been arrested so she went to the police. Told them she'd never even heard of you when they asked, and that she left Harding because he threatened to kill her."

"Oh, that poor woman!" Dana's hand flew to her mouth in horror.

"She's safe from him now," Drew put a comforting arm around her waist to hug her close, and Lex came in on the other side, bracketing her between them. "And so are you. He won't be getting out of jail for a long, long time."

She closed her eyes, savoring the warm, comforting embrace for a few moments before sighing. "I guess I could go back to my place then. There's nothing to be afraid of."

Both of them tightened their hold on her instinctively. "There isn't," Lex agreed, "but why do you have to go? Stay, Dana. We want you here. Both of us."

"You do?" She looked up at him, then at Drew, who nodded emphatically. "I don't — I don't want to mess up your relationship. You two have a great thing going, you're obviously happy together, I wouldn't want to get in the middle of that."

"Funny," Lex drawled, "because that's exactly where you fit best, angel."

She had to laugh, thumping him lightly on the chest. "You. You know that's not what I meant."

"We know," Drew cut in, "but we want you here, Dana. We've been looking for a third for a long time, someone who can accept who and what we are and who would be willing to be with both of us. Finding you seems like some kind of wonderful dream I don't want to end. Don't go. Stay with us."

There was nothing but sincerity in his blue-green eyes, and in Lex's bluer ones. Smiling up at both of them, Dana nodded. "Yes. Yes please."

"Good, that's settled," Lex said with a happy grin. "We're keeping you."

"Gah!" Dana made a face at him. "Maybe it's *me* keeping *you*," she said pertly.

"We'll discuss that when you can put either of us over your shoulder and carry us off to bed," Lex smirked.

"No!" Dana shrieked as he swooped. "Lex, you ass! I haven't finished my dinner!" she wailed, beating tiny fists on his back as he hauled her off to the bedroom, followed by a laughing Drew.

"It'll wait. We can heat it back up later," Lex put her down on the bed, grinning down at her.

"I'm hungry," she grumbled, but there was no sincerity in her voice and she started grinning as Lex and Drew both began stripping their clothes off, giving her quite a spectacular show. "Okay, maybe it can wait until later," she decided. "Much later…"

~ *The End* ~

DANA'S DUO

I hope you enjoyed reading *Dana's Duo* as much as I enjoyed writing it! Stay tuned for more sizzling action coming your way soon!

You can find my web page at caitlynlynch.com.

Scan the QR code below or visit http://eepurl.com/bPAElD to sign up to my mailing list. You'll be notified of my next sizzling hot publication and also get a chance to WIN amazing gifts and receive advance reader copies of my books to review!!

DANA'S DUO

www.ingramcontent.com/pod-product-compliance
Lightning Source LLC
Chambersburg PA
CBHW071004120726
47910CB00004B/1374